BRIDPORT PRIZE ANTH

EXTRACTS FROM THE NOVL

JUDGE
Emma Healey

First published in 2020 by Redcliffe Press Ltd
81g Pembroke Road, Bristol BS8 3EA

e: info@redcliffepress.co.uk
www.redcliffepress.co.uk
Follow us on Twitter @RedcliffePress

Follow The Bridport Prize:
Follow us on Twitter @BridportPrize
www.bridportprize.org.uk
www.facebook.com/bridportprize

ISBN 978-1-911408-75-8

British Library Cataloguing-in-Publication Data
A catalogue record for this book is available from the British Library

Typeset in 10.5pt Times

Typeset by Addison Print Ltd, Northampton
Printed by Hobbs the Printers Ltd, Totton

Contents

It's a long story

Writing a novel is like running a marathon, no matter what everyone tells you, it's best to go at your own pace. For those who cross the finish line, the next step is, now what?

That's where we come in. The Bridport Prize is the flagship of Dorset's Bridport Arts Centre and it began back in 1973. Almost fifty years later, it has grown into one of the most sought after writing prizes, attracting authors from across the globe.

In 2014, the Peggy Chapman-Andrews First Novel Award was established in honour of the Bridport Prize founder. It is run with commitment and in partnership with A.M. Heath Literary Agency, Tinder Press and The Literary Consultancy.

Beyond the prize

Our award winning alumni include Kelleigh Greenberg-Jephcott's *Swan Song* published in 2018 and chosen as one of *The Times* books of the year then long listed for the 2019 Women's Prize for Fiction.

Three of our winners are published this year in the UK, USA and the Commonwealth: Deepa Anappara's *Djinn Patrol on the Purple Line*, which was long listed for the 2020 Women's Prize for Fiction; Polly Crosby's *The Illustrated Child* and Stephanie Scott's *What's left of me is yours*. The *Observer* named both Deepa and Stephanie in their *10 Best Debut Novelists of 2020*.

We are tremendously proud of the part the Bridport Prize has played in discovering such innovative new writers. All our prize winners are proof that talent does indeed shine through. To the unknown writers who have a story to tell, please believe it could be you featured in these pages next year. Enjoy the extracts. We loved them.

The Bridport Prize Team
October 2020

Novel Award Partners

The Bridport Prize is proud to work in partnership with the following organisations in the delivery of the Peggy Chapman-Andrews Award for a First Novel.

A.M. Heath Literary Agents

Founded in 1919 by Audrey Heath and Alice May Spinks, two women who challenged the conventions of publishing, we are a London literary agency still very much driven by a passion to help writers who want to shift, shape or enrich the wider cultural conversation, and provide irresistible entertainment.

Championing our clients' writing remains at the heart of what we do. As well as a century of experience, we bring energy, ambition, and a keen eye for detail to our work.

We're always looking out for original ideas combined with great quality writing, and we work with the Bridport Prize to encourage emerging writers. By helping to draw up the long-list and shortlist for the Peggy Chapman-Andrews Award for a First Novel, we aim to support the best new novelists to find publishers and readers across the world.

Website: www.amheath.com
Twitter: @EuanThorneycrof / @AMHeathLtd

Tinder Press

Tinder Press is an imprint of Headline, which in turn is a division of Hachette – one of the largest publishing groups in the UK. Tinder Press was launched in 2013, and is Headline's home for literary fiction, a space where classy, intelligent writing can thrive. Our stable of prize-winning and bestselling authors includes Maggie O'Farrell, Andrea Levy, Patrick Gale, Deborah Moggach, Chloe Benjamin and Guy Gunaratne. Our authors have won or been listed for prizes including the Costa, Women's Prize, Dylan Thomas, Man Booker, Goldsmiths, Jhalak, Caine Prize, Orwell and Wellcome.

Tinder Press prides itself on its bespoke approach to publishing, which starts with an editor's passion, which then galvanises the whole publishing house. Our authors are always at the heart of everything we do, and our aim is to nurture their writing and build careers that will endure.

Website: www.tinderpress.co.uk
Twitter: Tinder Press / @maryanneharring

The Literary Consultancy
The Literary Consultancy is the UK's first and leading writing consultancy, offering editorial advice and manuscript assessment since 1996. Its aim is to provide honest, professional editorial feedback to writers to give them a better sense of whether and where their work might fit into the ever-changing market.

TLC and its team of world-class professional readers work with writers writing in English at all levels, across all genres. A popular 12-month mentoring programme, Chapter and Verse, supports writers to completion of a book project, alongside a suite of creative and practical events, and a yearly writing retreat, Literary Adventures.

The Literary Consultancy believes that fair, objective feedback can unlock the creative potential of writers at all levels, from emerging to professional. To achieve this, it focuses on cultivating the personal value of writing, equipping writers with the context, confidence, and skills they need to thrive and flourish.

Email: info@literaryconsultancy.co.uk
Website: literaryconsultancy.co.uk
Twitter: @TLCUK
Facebook: The Literary Consultancy

EMMA HEALEY

Judge's Report

What a year to judge a writing competition! A deadly virus, a global pandemic, world-wide protests, economic meltdown and wildfires. And I haven't even mentioned Brexit yet.

Maybe this accounts for the dark themes in the shortlisted entries. They featured characters whose lives were being turned upside down, characters who were losing their homes, friends, or sense of self, and who were looking for purpose, and struggling with loneliness.

The last theme is especially fitting considering that this year the judges couldn't meet in person, and that our conversation took place on Zoom (of course). I was wearing pyjama bottoms, we all got a good look at one of the judge's cartoon-animal-patterned curtains, and our soundtrack was a curious dog.

That didn't hold up proceedings, though. We had a lively discussion and talked about where we thought the novels would go after the thirty-thousand word mark, what was at stake in the stories, how true the characters' situations felt and whether the books delivered on the emotional promise and the bigger themes they were attempting to address.

Three of the entries were Highly Commended.

Mengo Baby has an intriguing premise. Isabel's search for meaning after her mother's death and the revelation that she has family she's never met and a past she knew nothing about promised a real adventure. We were all eager to explore the history and significance of the Indian population of Uganda, and the extract was full of lovely characterisation – we particularly enjoyed meeting Isabel's aunties.

Dog won the judges hearts with its touching depiction of a boy trying to pick his way through a bewildering and dangerous world. When Benjamin finds a greyhound on a local beach, and decides to keep it, he inadvertently makes a powerful enemy – his only ally a takeaway delivery driver with an anarchist streak. The dialogue was especially funny and clever, and the relationship between the two central characters uneasy and interesting. All the judges said we were keen to see what the author would write next.

The Silence Project was the most overtly political entry, grappling with mass protest movements and environmental activism as well as the rocky relationship between a mother and daughter. Emilia's mother has led twenty-one thousand women in a mass suicide pact, and has left her daughter with a collection of notebooks and a legacy of silence. Now Emilia must sift through the private records to find out who her mother really was. The extract juxtaposes an archivist structure with a coming of age story and the first shocking scene sets up a book that simmers with violence.

Our Runner Up was *The Cocklers*. A polished and well-composed entry about two very different protagonists. Harold and Su Lyn are both living in a northern English town but they'd hardly recognise it as the same place. One is angry at the way the world and his status has changed, the other is desperately trying to survive. It's a beautifully crafted story, not tricksy or showy, but really absorbing. All the judges loved Harold and felt he was someone we might meet on the street, and his conversations with his neighbour, Angela, created some great moments of humour and humanity. Resourceful and brave Su Lyn is someone you can't help rooting for. We wanted to know what would happen to these characters, and where the following chapters would take them.

Ultimately, we chose *Helen and the Fires* as our winner. The entry was ambitious in its scope, but sharp in its detail, full of surprises, beautiful observation and insights into the nature of story-telling. The writing is extremely stylish and was very much admired by all the judges. The protagonist, Helen, has decided to quit her job to write, but finds herself in the middle of an uncanny investigation into the self-immolation of three seemingly unconnected people. There is a sinister operator, an army of followers, lost relationships and strange clues, and our protagonist moves through the world unsure of what she's seeing, unsure even of herself. It felt like a book for our time.

JEFF ADAMS

Lilies of the Valley

Synopsis

This is the story of the Aberfan disaster of October 1966.

It is shown through the eyes of the Morrison family: Gramps, Moira and husband Idwyll, son Jack and daughter, Reba, aged 10. Idwyll is a union rep at the local NCB colliery, while Moira works at Woolworth, part time. The family live contently in the village.

One day disaster strikes. A slag heap collapses burying the school and killing 116 children, including Reba. Idwyll and Jack join in the rescue effort.

Everything changes. The loss of a child has a devastating effect on the family. Rows. Accusations of bad parenting. Grief morphs to anger. Anger almost rips the family apart. Idwyll frequents the pubs for solace while Moira is sedated.

Moira eventually summons up reserves of strength she never knew existed, because she can finally sense grief is tearing her family apart.

Moira and other villagers want the tip remains removed. Not only is it a reminder, but families – especially those with surviving children – fear it may happen again, especially when rain falls. The National Coal Board (NCB) advises everything is fine so Moira and Idwyll form a pressure group.

They invade the Welsh Office and dump tip slurry on the floor. Later, Idwyll is arrested for protesting in Aberfan with a placard denouncing the NCB and the Government for taking a huge chunk out from the Disaster Fund to remove the tip.

After a while, Moira and others form clubs to help depressed mothers, including sewing clubs and choirs.

Slow recovery but a recovery.

PROLOGUE
9.15 am FRIDAY 21st OCTOBER 1966.

Death never strays far from the valleys.

The mountains, mute witnesses of many a disaster, remain just that.

Atop Merthyr mountain, Tip 7 towers above the mining village, 600' below.

11

Volcanic-like, exhaling a sulphurous stench across the narrow valley like an invisible net.
When the weathervane spins and stops like a roulette ball, the wind scoops up wave after wave of coal dust scattering it across the valley like black sand.

Its black tentacles creep down the mountainside, burying the 4' high measuring pegs placed at its toes.
Advance it does.
Day in, day out.
The colliery never sleeps. Stoppage cost.

Mother Nature hates its hubris-thinking itself a mountain, so one day decides to teach it a lesson.
A lesson no-one will ever forget.
Death is on the rampage.
116 children are catapulted into Eternity.
A new word enters the Oxford Dictionary: ABERFAN: Disaster of the first magnitude.

CHAPTER 1
MERTHYR TYDFYL COUNCIL CHAMBERS
JANUARY 1964

Cigarette-grimed oil portraits of past mayors' frown down in the gloom of the council chamber.

'Any other business?'

The council leader, spectacles poised on the bridge of his nose, a woodbine clamped in his mouth, and an overflowing ashtray nearby, scans the chamber.

A silence ensues.

A shuffling of papers.

He glances at Cllr Williams, who has yet to speak.

Cllr Williams, prim and bespectacled, wife of "Slogar" Williams, retired headmaster, and JP.

'Mrs Williams, councillor for Aberfan and surrounds' announces a weary voice, aware that members already know who she is, but council procedures must be followed.

Facing fellow councillors with the air of a schoolteacher, she pauses for a moment, collects her thoughts.

Council members whisper conspiringly, glance at the wall clock, yawn.

The stenographer waits patiently, fingers poised.

The wall clock seems to tick louder by the second.

She coughs.

'Mr Chairman, fellow councillors, and the PRESS,' she said, nodding at the young man sitting in the PRESS section with his back to her. Upon hearing 'press' he turns about.

He had been observing a flock of bickering sparrows on the bare treetops outside.

A junior reporter for the local Merthyr Express newspaper, he's been covering council meetings since time immemorial, or so it seems, and if truth be told, mighty tired of them.

He longs for a huge scoop. But here in the valleys?

'I wish to know, Mr Chairman, what we propose to do about the potential danger that Aberfan's tip 7 poses? Should it collapse, then the schools further down will-do I have to spell it out?'

Council members exchange glances, nod or shake their heads, whisper. Silence ensues for a moment.

The wall clock seems to tick louder.

The Chairman nods at the Town Clerk who nods at his secretary who rises and coughs.

'Mr Chairman, Cllr Williams, I have here, a letter from the National Coal Board assuring us that the matter is indeed in hand.'

He proudly displays it, like Chamberlain returning from Munich after negotiating peace terms with Hitler. He read an extract from it and then passes comment.

'In short, the good people of Aberfan have nothing to worry about concerning tip 7. The NCBare, after all, experts in such matters, and perhaps Cllr Williams should show some faith in them?'

At that he sat down, looking rather pleased with himself.

A water jug leapt as a small fist came crashing down onto the table. Eyebrows rose. A chorus of tut tuts erupted.

The reporter stopped doodling and sat bolt upright, pen poised.

'The NCB do what they do best, 'she said sardonically, they give us false assurances! And I'm ashamed to say, certain members here, who really ought to know better, fall for their duplicity. They send letter after letter advising us that they the experts have it all under control.

The Coal Board receives our letters of complaint and then deposits them in their archives – which effectively bins them – that is if they have ever read them in the first place!

Until recently we have had several tip slides, the latest only a few months ago. Fortunately, there were no casualties.

I interpret this as a warning – a rehearsal of what is to come unless immediate action is taken.'

'Objection!'

A councillor stands up.

'The Town Clerk has advised us of what the NCB has said-what more does Cllr Williams want?

The NCB have advised that the matter is in hand – they are the experts after all, Cllr Williams.'

He sits down, shaking his head.

She continues.

'Fellow councillors,' she said glancing about the chamber, 'what's the point of their assurances, they are worthless. They hold meeting after meeting concerning our complaints, indeed, some of you here today have attended some and nothing comes out of them except yet more meetings!

Again, I remind you that the offending tip is some 600 feet high and contains a million tonnes of coal slag....'

'Thank you, Cllr Williams, your concerns have been noted,' said the Chairman, glancing at the clock.

'The next letter addressed to the NCB will indeed be stiffly worded. Any other business?'

'I will not let this go, Mr Chairman.'

He smiles weakly at her.

Cllr Williams sighs and sits down.

A brief conversation continues among the other councillors concerning the coming half-term holiday, then ceases.

Councillor Williams remains silent.

'This meeting I declare over.'

The reporter hastens out of the chamber. Councillors file out, cold air sweeps in.

Councillor Williams shivers.

CHAPTER 2
54 YEARS LATER
OCTOBER 21st 2016. 5Oth ANNIVERSARY OF THE ABERFAN DISASTER.

As the Merthyr train departs Merthyr Vale station, a silver-haired man, who has just got off, boarded the Aberfan bus.

It headed downhill, over the old colliery railway track, where it turned a sharp right, continuing along Nixonville road towards Aberfan.

To his left flows the silver thread of the river Taff thinly screened by trees, to his right, a vast wasteland stretching towards the far mountain, stony and barren of life, apart from a few wandering sheep and long tangled grass.

Rusty tram wheels peep through the grass like abandoned cannon wheels.

Here once stood the beating heart of Aberfan: the colliery.

The upper deck gave him a good view and he observed everything with a keen eye for he had once lived here.

Man against Nature. Hewing coal out of the bowels of the reluctant mountain had been hard dangerous work, and no amount of legislation could remove the dangerous environment.

Opposite the wasteland stood row after row of terraced houses that once clustered about the colliery. Behind them slugged the river Taff, prone to frequently flooding the miners' homes.

In his mind's eye he visualised the massive skeleton-like pithead structure with its huge, spinning wheels silhouetted against the scarred mountain, hear the steel cage's gate slam shut like the crashing of prison doors as men, caged sardine-like, plummet into the gaping inky abyss. The frantic hum of the spinning wheel as it dropped cage after cage into the hot, foul-breathed abyss. The thump thump thump of the fan.

The pit rarely slept. Stoppages cost.

Furious shouts, the clank of shunting coal-wagons connecting Coal-laden wagons hauled away by smoke-belching iron horses, file out from the colliery.

Gardeners wave at the passing convoy which responds with a shrill whistle and puff of smoke as it rattles along the rail track towards Cardiff docks, fuelled by the same black gold that once fuelled the British Empire.

Black faced miners pour out of the colliery, clothes cardboard stiff with sweat, chewing baccy, spitting black lung.

On pay days women wait for husbands outside the colliery gates before pub doors open. A forest of chimneys, surrounded by squat buildings, belch thick black smoke.

Hissing steam pipes, black oily puddles strewn across the colliery yard, massive cables coiled like pythons lay here and there. Everything is starved of colour. Rats scuttle under timbers.

Ghosts of the past, long gone.

A bell rang, the bus stopped.

The man got off opposite the red-bricked Mac Hotel.

It was a beautiful chilly morning. He headed up the short hill.

Arriving at the Memorial Garden he studied the place. It struck him as a little spooky.

The gate squealed as he opened it. A whirring noise, he glanced up: CCTV.

'Dear God!'

The camera began stalking him, a solitary figure, as he strolled across the Garden, acutely aware that he was walking on the very ground where once stood the stricken classrooms.

A shiver shot down his spine.

Pausing here and there to admire the Garden he looked up at the distant scarred mountains, mute witnesses to many a Welsh tragedy.

He pulled up his overcoat collar, a chill still in the air, or was the place getting to him?

He had seen enough after only a few minutes. It was time to visit the cemetery where lay his sister's remains.

She'd be about sixty now, he thought.

Outside the Garden he glanced up at the bronze plaque with the names of the dead in bold letters. His coal-blue scarred finger slid down the list stopping at MORRISON REBA aged 10.

A wave of melancholy swept over him as he lingered there. Alone, except for Cyclops.

He thought he could hear gulls screeching like lost souls. Then he could hear screaming, shouting, a ball banging. A cacophony of noises. Children running, skipping, hopping, a teacher's whistle blowing somewhere.

Then he saw them.

Scores of children inside the playground stood pressed up against the school railings, some sucking thumbs, watching him.

Close by stood several crates of milk bottles, some with tiny holes punched in them, evidence of early callers.

Behind the children stood the Victorian school, which threw out a ghostly yellowish light onto the playground.

Figures part as another child appears. Staring intently at him stood a pretty, blonde pig-tailed girl whom he recognised at once: his sister Reba. A smile of recognition crossed her face.

Their eyes locked for a moment.

Her hand reached out through the railings.

'Reba, little sister!'

He trembled.

Shouts. A whistle.

The image ebbed away.

Gone.

He fumbled for a handkerchief and blew his nose.

The camera nodded, returns to slumber.

CHAPTER 3

The sky darkened as inky coloured clouds mustered over the distant mountains and spread across the valley, shroud-like.

Gentle it began, a hesitant tap tap, barely audible. Then heavier, more persistent. Torrents of coal-dusted rainwater poured along rooftops, eddying down drainpipes and gushing onto the streets of Aberfan, flooding the drains.

From an end house of a long row of grime-covered miners' houses across the valley at Merthyr Vale, a telescope perched precariously on a window ledge, peeping gingerly out of an open bedroom window.

Coal dust strewn across the window ledge like sprinkled pepper, forming an inky substance as raindrops struck, streaking down the exterior wall.

Wind-driven rain whipped into the bedroom.

Behind the rickety telescope sat a schoolboy, still in his pyjamas.

Nearby on a table was a black and white school photograph of his classmates.

The telescope had a wide uninterrupted view, the historic town of Merthyr Tydfil to his right, five miles north.

To his left, Perthygleison, the top end of Aberfan.

Directly across the valley was Aberfan, with its long grids of terraced houses, drab streets, and coal-dusted sloping gardens. Chimneys smoking like snuffed candles.

Way below the house's rear garden ran the black thread of the Taff river, and running parallel to it the Merthyr-Cardiff railway line, rare it was they parted company for long, en route.

For several minutes the mist curled and uncurled, revealing gaps here and there. The telescope jerked aimlessly about seeking something of interest to focus on, for he wanted toimpress his butties presently ensconced at Pantglas Junior school.

It fixed upon the spent, old undulating tips carpeted in anaemic-looking grass. Here, during Summer months he spent many happy days playing cowboys and Indians.

Still searching, he was about to give up when something caught his eye across the valley.

Tip 7 towered menacingly above Aberfan, Vesuvius-like. It appeared out of the mist and then disappeared giving it an air of undeserved mystery.

A gust of wind suddenly caught its apex, flicking coal dust off like black sand.

He tweaked it up a notch bring tip 7 into focus and closer.

Something was amiss.

17

Figures atop the tip scatter.

Tip 7 had slipped, leaving its tram rails hanging over the edge, like a long accusing finger pointing towards the colliery from whence the coal slag had journeyed, two miles away.

A gigantic black mass was avalanching down the mountainside, disappearing into the mist, thundering towards the school.

The boy rubbed his eyes: was he imagining it?

Another peep through the telescope confirmed his suspicions.

'Pooh!' said the boy, his face contorting, as sulphurous gases spread across the valley floor.

Horror was unfolding before his very eyes.

The distance between the avalanche and school was shrinking fast. Then his face lit up: this could mean only one thing, he thought, no school for some time!

'Dew dew,' he said, 'wait till I tell my butties,' not realizing he'd never see them alive again.

The bedroom door burst asunder. Deep in concentration the boy was totally oblivious of his mother's presence.

'Why aren't 'ewe dressed ready for the doctor's bach?'

His face flushed. The telescope collapsed.

'Agh! My floor.'

His face turned crimson.

'My rug is soaking wet. Wait till 'ewe father comes home, now then!'

The bedroom door slammed shut, the wall shook.

Atop Tip 7 colliery workers scramble for safety. The mountain of coal slag trembles violently as if throttled by giant hands. Its apex sinks twenty feet or more, rises and overflows like rogue dough.

Both queuing trams, overladen with coal waste, and tram rails edge over the tip edge, plummeting into the black abyss.

The now unsupported mass, like a burst dam, explodes, plunging down the steep mountainside. Quickly gaining momentum, it touches speeds of 60 mph, with an ear-splitting intensity. A giant heaving black mass towering fifty feet high or so. A battering ram, thundering down the valley slopes scooping up huge boulders, trees, telegraphpoles; the latter snap like twigs.

A black Tsunami tidal wave.

A short row of farmhouses directly in its path, crumble upon impact, instantly killing itsoccupants.

Sheep scatter. Feeding birds directly in its path, explode into the air.

Bursting through the enshrouding mist halfway down the mountainside, roaring like a giantbeast, it pummels the ground, ravaging everything in its path.

Farmhouse chickens surf the tidal waves momentarily before sinking. Incredulously, some survive.

Escaping gases ignite spouting fire.

In a nearby pond cattle sunk to their hocks cease drinking and look up. Then resume drinking.

The seething mass heaves over the Old Canal Bank, a disused railway track. Momentarily it pauses as if unsure of its direction, but then spirals right with a mighty roar.

The school braces itself.

TATUM ANDERSON

Mengo Baby

Synopsis

Mengo Baby, *a contemporary literary novel, tells the story of a woman who sets about uncovering secrets her dying mother kept from her. She travels to Uganda and discovers deep racial divides that challenge her own identity, against the backdrop of Idi Amin's reign of terror.*

Isabel's only close blood relation and rock, her mother Helen, is dying. But when Isabel reaches the hospice to say goodbye, she finds three women claiming to be mother's cousins. They have brought a priest to perform the last rites though Helen has been vehemently non-Catholic for as long as Isabel can remember. It turns out, her mother asked them to come. And Helen isn't even her mother's real name.

She discovers that her mother's family was part of the wave of Asians thrown out of Uganda in the early 70s. Isabel has become part of a culture she never knew.

When Helen dies, Isabel discovers an engagement ring that her mother has carried for years, one not given by her father. Isabel, recently divorced, with a career in tatters, feels rootless after Helen's death. She decides to find the man her mother loved and why her mother rejected her own family.

Isabel travels to Uganda for answers. She uncovers a city so ingrained in its colonial past that the separation of the races is reflected in the very streets and houses.

Isabel eventually finds the man who loved her mother and uncovers tensions between Europeans, Asians and Africans that made mixed-race children, like her, taboo. Isabel finally grapples with the meaning of roots, loyalty and belonging. Importantly, she discovers what family and kinship means to her.

Chapter 1

The day she was supposed to die, there should have been rain so heavy my clothes sucked cold to my skin. When I ran for the bus that would take me to see her, I should have missed it. A pall of exhaust should have choked me as the bus pulled away. But of all the days to be sparkling, with dazzling summer light and trees a brash, loud kind of green, it had to be this one.

It was hot at the bus stop and hotter on the bus. I searched for a seat near an open window, passing a man in headphones laughing in short breathy explosions while wiping tears from his eyes. I chose a seat next to a quiet woman dressed in a glittery t-shirt, holding a phone and swiping through pictures of dogs.

The toddler sitting in the seat opposite began a song.

'*The wheels on the bus go round and round, round and round,*' she sang.

She was dressed in shorts with shiny plastic sandals that banged against the seat while she sang. My eyes followed her small arms, twirling like the wheels of the bus. I willed those preposterous blonde curls and porcelain skin, thieved from some Victorian children's book, off the bus.

But no, the song, in half-formed speech, and the banging of her feet carried on. Dribble began to rope from her mouth.

I felt inside my rucksack for headphones. But I found only a toothbrush, toothpaste and two empty crisp packets. Chalky blue beads of dried toothpaste and crumbs stuck to my fingers. The headphones I had left at home.

I swore behind gritted teeth, too loudly. The little girl started with big eyes. She stared at me, the thick saliva still dangling from her wet chin. Tuts came from the seat behind.

A woman, I guessed must be the Mother, was sitting beside the toddler, all long and preened and glossy-haired. I studied her, and her pregnant bump and the way she placed the child on her lap, facing her, with a beatific smile. Without a glance at me, the woman lent towards the child and began to sing the next verse.

'*The mummies on the bus say shush shush shush,*' sang the woman.

She placed a long finger on her lips as she sang: '*Shush, shush, shush.*'

The child joined in, her padded, nappied bottom bobbing up and down on the Mother's lap. And then the Mother flashed me a look. It was quick but I caught its full force.

I looked down at my phone screen, hoping for a distraction from this nauseating maternal scene, this relentless rhyme. There were piles of messages.

On the day she was supposed to die, I refused to spend a single second on people who thought a digital message replaced a visit to a dying woman. I could see clearly, today, who was worth my time. I deleted them one by one, my finger slapping the screen hard.

The more messages I deleted, the more I could see of my mum, smiling there on the home screen. She was always smiling even when there was nothing to bloody well smile about. I hadn't inherited her optimism, that's for sure. That's what she always said. Maybe I got it from Dad, I'd reply. There'd be a flicker across her face and she would say, maybe.

On the day my mum was supposed to die, the Mother and child were onto the next verse.

'*The grannies on the bus go chatter chatter chatter.*' They squeezed their fingers together and apart like quacking ducks' beaks. Other passengers cooed at the toddler. She was climbing down from her mother now, retrieving a bucket and spade from a bag on the floor.

They were probably on the way to the seaside. It was hot enough. Mum used to take me to Margate on days like this. I remember the outfit I wore once, the one with matching yellow shorts and zip up top with red beading. We waited for the bus when it was still cold, first thing. Mum made egg mayo sandwiches, and put me on those double swings they still have on the beach. I don't remember what else was there in Margate, just lots of people and heat and sand beneath my toes and candy floss on long wooden sticks that fizzed on my tongue.

The sand whipped through my hair, I remember that. I don't know how she got it out. I had an Afro then. It must've been a nightmare. But she was always gentle with my hair. She washed it, combed it and oiled it well. But I always wanted it slicked back like other girls. For years I wondered how they managed to make every single strand of hair lie flat on their heads. I didn't know that was called relaxing back then, that it was chemicals that made their hair shiny, straight and smooth. I'm sure she didn't either. She let it look like Dad's, a halo of fuzz around my head, in school photos.

We would sit on the sand while Mum unpacked the sandwiches from an old ice cream box, the kind that stank of plastic. She never put meat in the sandwiches, in case it got too hot and I got ill. She always packed a Penguin. It was the only time we had shop-bought snacks, when we went to the seaside. I washed down my lunch with warm sweet orange squash from an old rinsed out water bottle. While I swallowed, my fingers felt for the glue, still tacky from where she'd ripped off the label. The sea swished and swashed. Margate was a lifetime ago and we'd never go again.

My lips were cracked. I licked them with my tongue. The Mother was taking long sips from a glistening water bottle, rubbing her bump, flaunting it. When she finished, she screwed the lid shut, and reached for a wet wipe and moved towards the child's face.

'Freya darling, let mummy wipe your face,' said the Mother. The child wriggled her head away from the woman's fingers and screeched. The screams almost pierced me. Just then, the bus reached a bus stop. I grabbed my rucksack and ran off.

I cursed myself the minute the bus sped off, the wheels going round and round, taking the child and her bucket and spade and the Mother in the direction of the hospice faster than I could get there.

My stomach tightened. I now saw the better version of me, the one with the patience for a singing toddler, the one who stayed on the bus and got there just in time to hold my mother's hand as she passed, passed away, passed over, or whatever the euphemism was. And here was me, the worse version as usual, running breathless and hungover and crying under my breath towards the hospice.

I dashed for the crossing, while the neon seconds counted down, three, two, one.

She could be dying right now, all by herself.

I ran as fast as I could, the heat filling my lungs. Sweat pricked in my armpits and between my legs, unconditioned from months of staying by my mother's bedside.

She could be dead, now.

I looked down at myself, as I ran. My clothes were wrong for this superheated summer. My jumper was still encrusted with splashes of last night's dinner, eaten fast and dog-tired in front of the TV. I knew I shouldn't have done the bottle of wine too. But the worst version of me needed it.

The call came around nine this morning. I answered it, my voice thick with sleep, still lying in my clothes on the sofa.

'Trish, she alright?' I said.

'Iz, I think you probably need to come in my love,' said Trish. She was the nurse who was on when Mum was admitted two weeks ago.

'God. But she seemed settled when I left.'

'I know. I'm afraid she didn't have a great night. We called you a bit earlier but I think you must have needed to sleep,' she said. Her voice was calm and matter-of-fact. 'She's comfortable now, don't worry. But I thought you'd probably want to be here.'

'Thanks Trish,' I said. 'I'm on my way. Tell her to hang on.'

'I will,' said Trish. 'Though there's a bit of a crowd here now.'

'A crowd?'

'Yes,' she said. 'Her cousins.'

After Trish's call, I had a quick shower. Under the falling water, I tried to work out which cousins they could be. Mum did not talk to her family. There were two brothers in Canada and a sister still living at the family home in Goa. I met her when we visited my grandfather when I was very small. I did not remember anybody else.

If anyone came to see my mum, it was Dad's family. My stepbrother Patrick, Auntie Madge. Mum's closest friend Carole, sat with her regularly so I could show my face at work. There was George, her boss and a few of the old neighbours who popped in, though they no longer knew what to say. Mum had greyed and shrunken. The cousins must be Dad's. There were many of them.

I scraped my hair back after my shower and searched for clean clothes. There were so few, I put on the jumper from yesterday. It smelled of armpits and onions and disinfectant. The state of me. But I couldn't make myself care enough about washing clothes, work or summer, even if Mum could smell me through the haze of dying and morphine.

Far off down the high street, drenched in sunshine, I could see the bus reach the bus stop without me. And then it sped off in the direction of the seaside.

I kept running. The world was about end, but all around me were smiling people in sunglasses that sparkled, the sound of laughter and clinking of cups at pavement cafes.

By the time I reached the hospice, I could barely breathe. I took the lift to the ward bent over double the whole way. I pressed the buzzer long and hard, announced myself through the intercom and squirted too much antiseptic foam onto my hands. I waited, my head leaning against the double doors to Mum's ward, daring them both to open. The buzzer sounded.

I took a deep breath and held it as I pushed one door open and walked past the nurse's station, the toilets, the visitor's sitting area, the stacks of mattresses by one wall, three nurses and all the many doorways to different rooms that came off the main corridor until I reached Mum's.

And there it was, the sound of her rasping breath coming from inside the room. I exhaled. I forgave the child, the Mother, the bus and the whole world. Mum was still here.

J M BRISCOE

The Girl with the Green Eyes

Synopsis
The Girl with the Green Eyes, *part one of a soft science fiction trilogy, tells the story of* **Bella D'accourt** *both as a child coming to terms with her own controversial origins and as an adult on the run with her daughter. Bella is a 'designer baby' – her parents paid for her to be given a set of predominant genes, in Bella's case, beauty and grace. When she is nine Bella's mother brings her 'back' to the scientists behind the programme,* **Dr Frederick** *and* **Ana Blake***, after Bella uses her manipulative charm to seriously injure another child. Bella is taken in by the Blakes and soon begins to take a role in their new eugenic project designed to push the boundaries of human possibility.*

In 2018, Bella and daughter **Ariana***, 12, go into hiding after Bella is tracked down by her former friends, including* **Ralph Blake***, her surrogate brother. Bella is not scared of Ralph, but she is terrified that his finding her means she will also be discovered by* **Josiah Lychen***, a former colleague of Dr Blake's who began to show an interest in Bella when she was 14. Bella's fears are realised when Ariana is kidnapped by Lychen and used as bait to lure Bella to one of Lychen's laboratories where his eugenic research has taken a sinister turn, including the creation of a servile army whose humanity has been removed.*

Ralph, who believes he is Ariana's father, goes with Bella to rescue Ariana. A flashback reveals Lychen raped Bella 13 years ago. Bella trades Ariana's freedom for her own. Lychen wants her to work with him. He believes he loves her, but Bella knows he regards her as a possession. Bella relinquishes custody of Ariana to Ralph so no one discovers Lychen is actually her father.

The Girl with the Green Eyes
Summer, 2005
'I won't wait forever, Bella,' Lychen murmured, and as I began to move away he struck, clenching a fistful of my hair and jerking my entire upper body backwards. It lasted less than a second. Less than a second and less than a twinge of pain and imbalance, but the warning rang clear between us; with one flex of his arm he could throw me backwards onto the soft

carpet and wrench away everything I held so precariously from him. As I jolted upright, Lychen turned back to the desk and casually picked up his wine glass. I took three steps across the carpet.

'Sooner or later you're going to have to choose a side, Bella.'

I kept walking.

'Before the choice is taken from you.'

I didn't reply. I didn't trust my voice. Instead, when I reached the door I turned and looked at him. He lowered his glass and licked the wine from his lips, his eyes blazing into me as hard as they had when he'd gripped my hands. I turned and ran.

I didn't feel my heels. I didn't register the frenzy of my heart juddering my entire ribcage under the flimsy silk of my shirt. I didn't think about where I was going. I didn't even notice the tears, cold against the warmth of my face, until Ralph looked up, his eyes widening in surprise.

'What the–? Beast? Are you OK? Are you *crying?*'

'No,' I said reflexively as I shut the door behind me and waited, my hand upon it, until I was sure. Until *he* definitely hadn't followed me. He wouldn't. Not here.

'You *are*,' Ralph was behind me, too near, and when he put his hand on my shoulder to peer more closely at my face I flinched violently.

'Woah, sorry,' he held up his hands. I stood alone, chest heaving, heart hurting, trying with everything I had to control it all, to cool it all down but it was all wrong. My face was red, the worst colour for a face to be. My armpits were damp and the silk shirt was clinging to my body. My hair felt scattered and wrong where Lychen had grasped it. I stared around at the laboratory to try and calm myself down. It was dark, the only light coming from the lamp hovering over the same work area Ralph had been using that morning, the two text books still open but at a further point now, I could see. No one else was here. Outside, darkness had finally overtaken the heavy twilight and the cool air from the open window lapped at the heat tumbling from me like chaos.

'What's happened to you?' Ralph's hair was still sticking up, he'd lost his lab coat and rolled the sleeves of his checked shirt up, but he still bore sweat patches beneath his raised arms. He looked as discombobulated as if one of the red deer we sometimes spotted from the ARC's western windows had just leapt through the door.

And do you blame him? You never *lose control like this. Calm down. Nothing happened.*

'Nothing happened,' I echoed in a mutter, bringing a shaking hand up to try and smooth my hair back into place. As I did so I realised my palms were stinging. I brought them down and saw tiny crescents of blood embedded across the soft pads beneath my thumbs. I closed my fists but Ralph was too quick. He took my hands in his large ones and gently prised them open.

'Who did that?'

'Nobody. I must have done it myself... I was watching the kids rehearse earlier... I got nervous, you've seen Nova do that big swoop through the fire...'

'Bella. I've heard you coach the kids – you told Nova last week that you'd ordered extra-flammable feathers for her costume to make sure she flew straight through the fire hoops and didn't keep arching her back in mid-air. Besides, we both know you'd sooner trek through the moor out there in your designer heels than do something to disfigure yourself in some way... It was Lychen wasn't it?'

'It– he... it was *nothing*...' I said all in a whoosh, and suddenly Ralph's arms were around me and the smell of him, sweaty but safe, was in my nose and to my horror I could feel the tears coming properly this time, like a surging hurricane devouring everything in its path. *Robots don't* – but it was too late. My self-control crumpled like a house made of sticks.

I don't know how long we stood there; him just wrapped around me, cocooning my shudders and sobs until they slowly began to subside. I didn't care that he was supposed to be like a brother to me, or that only that morning I had wanted to hurt and humiliate him as much as I ever had. He didn't say anything, even when I stopped sobbing and pointed out, in a muffled, shaky voice most unlike my own, that really, nothing *had* happened. I'd been offered a new job. That was it. Really.

'Not *really* really, though, is it?' He said, gruffly. I looked up. His eyes were there – brown, solid, waiting. 'I *warned* you about him. Mamma tried to warn you... He won't stop, he won't ever let you go until he–'

I kissed him. I don't know what made me do it, but I know it *was* me – even if it was just a small, impetuous part of me that I'd kept buried for years – that decided. That reached my body upwards and found his lips with my own. Maybe I was grateful to him for providing me with what I'd needed to claw my way back into myself. Maybe it was the only way I could think of to answer him, to *choose my side*, as Lychen had put it. Or perhaps I simply wanted him to shut up.

October, 2018

'Run, Ariana! Ralph, *go!*' My words strangle from my throat as another explosion shatters the air with dust. Shapes move uncertainly across the room as I'm pulled backwards. Another icy limb wraps around my chest and suddenly I know who has me and I can't breathe, let alone reach for the blade in my pocket. The blackness of memory swells within me until it reaches my throat and my eyes, blotting out everything but the cold hardness choking me from all angles. I try to inhale and my lungs flounder weakly, there is a hard surface pressing into my face and pain clenches like a knife, reaching for my softest parts and wrenching them inside out.

I don't know if I pass out. I don't know if hours pass or mere seconds, but eventually the snake around my ribcage eases and a tiny parcel of oxygen filters through my lips. Then a tiny bit more. And then I blink and can see the dark shadow of the table, the empty spaces where Ariana, Ralph and the woman have fled. Nothing is pressing into my face. Nothing is knifing me. And, slowly, Lychen's arm loosens until it's merely a chain around me.

'Be still,' he croons, too close, and when I flinch he tightens his hold again until I obey. 'Good... Just relax. You're fine...'

We're alone in the room. The dust has begun to clear, only shimmering a little with the bangs that have become distant. He is behind me, holding me with one arm while the other slowly twists my wrist up in between my shoulder blades. As I realise it, my shoulder gives a sudden yawn of pain and I gasp.

'It hurts, doesn't it?' He remarks placidly, and I shudder again as *that* memory, so spectrally close, threatens to take over once again.

'Yes,' I gasp. He sighs slowly and I can feel how much he's enjoying himself. I can't see his lips but I know they are moist with the pleasure of dominance, his tongue flickering over them like a serpent's. He shifts a little so I can feel the cold knuckle of the handgun at his hip.

'I'll let you go if you promise not to run.'

'Fine.'

'Good girl,' he sighs into my neck and I feel his lips graze me there for a second just before his grip loosens and the pain in my shoulder retreats. I stumble forward, coughing as my desperate lungs suck in the debris-laden air around us. More distant bangs drift into the room as I grasp the back of an ornately carved chair for support.

'Well, well,' Lychen mutters, striding around to the head of the table. I cough into my hand and look up at him. His face is more animated than it used to be; or perhaps I've simply forgotten how he looks when something surprises him.

'It seems, once again, that I have underestimated you. Or at least one of you...'

'I don't...' I cough and he passes me a bottle of water from a side table. I take it because there's no sense in not being able to speak. The water is like cool nectar on my scorched throat. I remember, suddenly, that there is a knife in my pocket.

'I don't understand,' I say, evenly.

'Let's just say these little bangs we're hearing aren't fireworks I put on for your benefit. Not that I'm not pleased to see you, of course.'

'What is it, then? What's going on?'

Keep him talking. Give them a chance to get away. Ralph can handle the Guard. Maybe. This is Ariana's biggest threat, right here.

'My best guess is that a small band of vigilantes from the ARC followed you here and are attempting to... ah... rescue you. They're no match for my Guard, of course... But I would have given them a slightly less *bangy* greeting had I known they were to join us... Which begs the question of how they managed to thwart our tracking software...'

'I've no idea,' I say drily, my eyes skirting from him to the door behind him and back around to the one through which we entered.

'No... It's more Bryden's style, isn't it... But *how* could she have accessed our system remotely... Unless...'

More bangs sound and this time they're closer again. Heavy footsteps pause only briefly outside the door before pounding on. Shouts rip through the air. I think I recognise Felix's voice, twisted in anger and pain.

'Well. I shall be able to ask Ms Bryden soon enough, by the sound of things,' Lychen smiles coldly. 'So let us proceed while we have some semblance of privacy.'

'Proceed?' I tear my eyes away from the door, swallowing hard against the flutter of panic in my stomach. Lychen is holding Blake's report, which now wears a fine layer of dust.

'Don't you want to know why I went to so much trouble to track you down through your hapless child?'

He brushes the papers clean and taps them gently against one of his white, glistening teeth.

'I presume it's to do with the demise of the other A Subjects,' I say as more blasts echo into the room. I'm still holding the chair, my body carefully angled so he doesn't see me reach into my pocket for the knife. Keeping my eyes locked on his, I ease it slowly out of its sheath and slide it up my sleeve.

'Partly, yes.'

'Go on, then. Am I dying? Am I *defective* like my mother said all along? Don't keep me in suspense.' I screw the sarcasm into my words even as I realise, to my own surprise, that at this particular moment I really don't give a damn what those pages say.

'You're fine,' Lychen says softly, looking at the papers and then up at me. The old, wolfish flames stir into his dead eyes. 'You're perfect, in fact.' He moves closer. 'As ever you were...'

'But it could change any moment,' I say, quickly. 'Look at what happened to my brother. He was fine too, then boom.'

As if in support of my point, the room gives another shake. Someone shouts thickly nearby. I shut my eyes for a second and hope with every particle of my being that Ralph has Ariana somewhere safe. When I open my eyes again Lychen is closer still and his hand is reaching and once again I get a flash of that hardness, that terrible, unyielding pain just as he brushes his fingers into the hair by my right ear.

'Bella... You know why I brought you here. You *must* know. It's not because of this,' he throws the report onto the table. 'That was just... a means to an end. A justification. To myself as much as anyone. I know you think me cold. Monstrous even, perhaps. And I've undoubtedly given you reason in the past.' His fingers find my neck like they never left. I shut my eyes again as nausea shudders through me. I can't move.

'But the truth is... Ever since I first met you when you were little more than a child, wearing a clean, white dress and gazing at me with such pure, unblemished beauty... I haven't been able to look at anything the same way. Bella... You make me weak in a way I never thought a human being could. I need you. I love you.'

My eyes snap open and I raise the blade to his neck in one swift movement. He blinks as he feels the cool metal press into his skin.

'You don't love or need anyone, Lychen,' I hiss, mustering everything to keep my voice level. 'You *want* me, perhaps...'

He frowns. 'What's the difference?' His hand falls from my throat, eyes flickering between me and the knife under his chin.

'Everything,' I whisper.

Now, the voice murmurs. *Do it now, before he remembers he has a gun.* He's furrowed in confusion and my mind shudders as the memory crowds in again. *Use it.* His hands on my head, slamming it forward. *Make him pay.* My own desk a cold slab against my cheek like a butcher's counter. *Make him bleed.* His fingers at my throat, squeezing the scream from my body. His other hand busy wrenching my clothes aside. And pain. Deep and knifing and crushing in every possible way. *Do it now.*

I push the knife upwards and Lychen gasps as a ruby gleam shivers onto the blade... There's a crash, the floor shivers beneath us and the door bursts open. It's a second of distraction but it's all Lychen needs to knock the knife out of my hand. It skitters across the table in front of us and I look up to see smoke, and Ethan, half his face swelling and bloody but wearing the beginnings of a grin as he takes a step towards us and turns to shout behind him. And Lychen glances over, raises his gun and shoots him in the chest.

SPENCER BUTLER

Pegwell Bay

Synopsis

Pegwell Bay *is set between 1858 and 2013; and moves between London, Dorset and Kent, with excursions to Montana, New York and Milan. It is about sexual orientation and identity. It is about the adherence to class and its trammelling; the seeking of truth in matters of love and the discovery of lies and betrayal; and the pleasure of being unique, the pain of secrecy, and the fear of exposure. Throughout, there hovers the invisible presence of unwritten rules, shifting and changing through the years; and of expectations that must be adapted with every experience that bubbles up before evaporating.*

For Terence, things are not as they appear: events turn out not to have happened in the way he has been led to believe; people are not who they say they are and pretence is used as a smokescreen to conceal the truth. This story is narrated by Terence, and his three lovers: Roland in the 1950s, Nick in the 70s, and Joe in the 90s. It observes these men's lives – and those of the men they encounter – and depicts the clandestine nature of their relationships – their loves, their denials and their disappointments – and the shifting experience of being gay; for a man from Ancient Greece to the men in the time of AIDS.

For Terence, his will be a life expressed in the only way he can; through painting. It will be a life spent searching for a truth that will not arrive until it is too late; and a life spent searching for meaning with his lovers, and with his family, too, whose contradictory story is narrated by a witness to their lives – Tommy, their biographer – and moves backwards in time, to 1894, and a revelation, as the story comes to a close, that will destroy them all.

1
Terence: At First
1928

I am five years of age. Or so I shall calculate, later in life, when I attempt to recall my first memories. Perhaps I shall be informed of these recollections by others, in their need to give shape and meaning, if not veracity, to my early days. Will it be my mother – Hesione – who kindly lets it be

31

known that my first memory was of being chased around a rose bed by a screaming, lurching being ten times my size and covered in white hair? Will it be my father – Lionel – who reminds me that the lurching hairy being was my grandfather – Cuthbert – and that the rose bed around which I was being chased was oval in shape and surrounded by lush grass that was cool to the touch of my dancing feet? Will he inform me that this took place in the garden of the house he and my mother – together with Miss Hampton, Mr. and Mrs. Cooper, Nel, George and Ralph – occupied at Young Street in Kensington; and that the roses looked for all the world as if they were made of purple crêpe paper – like the Archbishop of Canterbury – and gloried in the name of *Robert Le Diable*? Do I remember correctly the lilies, lupins, agapanthus, foxgloves and acanthus that stood to attention in the borders nearby; thrilled and excited by the ringing screams of delight that emanated from me and my lumbering pursuer? Or was I informed of this too, in passing, by my mother, or my father or Nel or George or Ralph? Perhaps, along the way, I might have stopped to contemplate which version of my life I would eventually lead; theirs or mine.

* * *

Today is my father's fiftieth birthday. My mother has decided we shall celebrate with a small party in the garden. An embroidered cloth and napkins, together with glasses and knives, forks and spoons, have been taken out and placed, by Nel, on a table set beneath the mulberry tree at the far end of the garden, and Mrs. Cooper has laid out sandwiches, pies and pickles, and a sponge cake with strawberries and cream.

My grandfather has arrived. For some reason I am too small to fathom my mother has chosen this day, amidst the hubbub in the house, to stop me half-way down the stairs – while I am carrying some bunting I have found in a trunk in the box room – to inform me that my grandfather is, in her opinion, the kindest man she has ever encountered, and that I must ignore any *froidure* that I might sense between him and my father. I wonder why she needs to tell me this as it only forces me to recall that whereas my mother refers to my grandfather as 'Cuthbert' it is my father who refers to him as 'your father-in-law' when speaking to my mother, and 'your grandfather', when talking to me. In fact, if I really ponder it, I cannot recall my father ever referring to his father as 'father', or 'Cuthbert', or anything else at all. I remember wishing I knew what *froidure* meant.

Apparently, whenever my grandfather's business requires him to be in London he leaves *Pegwell Bay* – the house in Kent where every claimant to the estate has been born – to sojourn for two weeks at the apartment my father's brother keeps at *Albany*, Piccadilly. Meanwhile Frederick – my father's brother – decamps, as my grandfather puts it, to *Spedding*, his country house in the southwest. It may seem contrary that I should refer to my uncle as 'my father's brother', but that is the manner in which he is distanced by everyone, especially my grandfather; and even by my father, too, if truth be told. Uncle Frederick is never present whenever my grandfather is at hand – neither here, there nor anywhere – and it would seem my father, for the safe and harmonious conduct of their various relationships – and, who knows, for my wellbeing – retains and encourages this arrangement and its accompanying merry-go-round of cross-country house swaps. My father responds to my questioning about his brother with what appears a pained but practiced exactitude, but always appears *uncomfortable* in doing so. My ignorance will remain bliss until the time in later life when someone – but not my grandfather, my father or my father's brother – will feel it is *necessary* to enlighten me.

Poor Pa-pa. He sits at one end of the table under the mulberry tree looking dejected – even though it is his birthday – watching my grandfather and me cavorting in the garden. He is unable to join us because a club-foot, with which he has been cursed since birth, makes it impossible, he says, for him to run in a straight line and at any speed that would engender the kind of mirth he thinks would please me. I try to suggest that straight lines are not required for chasing me round an oval rose bed, but this only brings a watery, distant smile to his face.

Later that afternoon Ralph drove us – my grandfather, my father and me – across Hyde Park to Selfridge's. My father had arranged, as a treat for his birthday, for us to be photographed; informing us he wished to somehow preserve memories of my growing up. By the way he fussed around my grandfather and pretty-well pushed him into the motor, together with his luggage, I could not help thinking perhaps he wished to preserve some memories of his own father too, but in a manner guaranteed to unnerve him. The *Photomaton* photo booth had arrived from Boston – unveiled the previous week on the lower ground floor of the store – and resembled the kind of bathing machine my grandfather says his wife used to enjoy at Margate in their younger days. We each took turns, directed by my father, to sit in the wooden box while it flashed and grunted about us. Or maybe the grunting emanated from my grandfather as he complained from within the curtained box that in his day a portrait by Leighton or Whistler or Sargent was good enough for *his* father. If anything, the grunting and complaining increased as my father pushed and pulled us into various father and son combinations dictated by seniority –

my grandfather and father first, then my father and me – and finally erupted into agitated whispered asides between my grandfather and father when he attempted to jam us all into the booth for a culminating dynastic snapshot. 'Your brother would have something to say about this,' I remember my grandfather complaining and, despite a half-smile of, I suppose, reassurance from my father, I couldn't help but agree that it would have been impossible to cram four of us into the tiny booth, even if my uncle had been in attendance and not motoring to Dorset.

There was a strained, embarrassed silence between us as we awaited the photographs; while other visitors to the store steered clear of us, and the *Photomaton* photo booth; and a uniformed major-domo hovered close by ready, from the stance he assumed, to step in and keep the peace, if required. My grandfather had wandered off, huffing and clucking, leaving my father and me to wait. After what seemed an eternity I found myself clutching the photographs. I was strangely spellbound by the images before me: three gentlemen of varying ages, bulk and height – but identically dressed – captured in degrees of blacks and greys and sepias, staring balefully and unsmiling out at me, looking for all the world like strangers. Whilst those of my father and me did betray a kind of closeness and affection I couldn't help but feel that those of my father and grandfather had a detachment – despite my father's smiles and cajolings – that belied what I knew of them both. At the same time, studying the photographs more closely created in me a suspicion that it was in the *images*, rather than the reality, that the truth about any *froidure* between them was more likely to be found.

I little realised at the time that this moment would develop and engrave itself on my mind, and remain with me for the rest of my life. It would lead me into a life of painting: putting down in oils on canvas what I saw and what I knew; what I felt and what I hoped for; and the contradictions, the joys and the disappointments that would entwine themselves around all my efforts. It was portraiture at first, then abstract works from Nature, and photo-montage. It would lead me, in 1941, to the Slade School of Art; to a meeting in my second term with Tommy – the longest and, up to a point, closest of my acquaintances – who became the Witness to all our lives. It would lead to a love affair with Duncan Grant that lasted for a week – in a hotel in Positano – until a Mister Keynes turned up unexpectedly to ruin everything. It would take me to Victoria Station, in 1955, where I would wait patiently for Francis as he thrashed and grimaced inside a photo booth, collecting evidence for the *Screaming Heads* he was about to paint; before toddling off to the gentlemen's lavatory to gather more, as he put it, 'raw material'. In 1960, it would lead to my first major exhibition, at the Redfern Gallery, in London.

We caught up with my grandfather at *Albany*. He must have trudged out of Selfridge's and commandeered the motor; ordering Ralph to drive on regardless of the fact that my father and I were missing. Ralph would have attempted a mild pantomime of wondering where The Master might be, only to be reminded by my grandfather that he was The Master's Master.

I could sense a dark silence hanging like a shroud around the pictures and chandeliers in the *Salon* when we finally entered the room. My grandfather had positioned himself in a blazing flame-stitched wing-backed armchair at one end of the room, clutching a Gin and French; his oiled beard glistening and bristling; his eyes darting from one part of the room to the other, but not at us. His chest was heaving as if he had sprinted through Mayfair in place of being driven by Ralph; who was standing to attention nearby, silver tray in hand, suddenly promoted from Chauffeur to Butler. Nothing was said. My grandfather stared impassively past us, his bulk constrained by tweed and resentment, looking for all the world like our good King, George the Fifth.

A child is free of the reasons why this disruptive adult behaviour occurs. A child can ignore the indignation that swirls about the room; and the silences; and the vacuums in which new misunderstandings and mis-interpretations can breed and bubble up and take hold of one's memories. A child – this child – moved from his father's side to wander from the deadness of the unfathomable room.

I have entered an ante-room in the shape of an eight-sided tent. Or so I will remember sometime in the future when Tommy and I come to research my uncle's life; particularly his time upon the battlefields of the Great War. The room is hung with blood-red linen; and the ceiling is draped to a centre point where a steel lantern hangs. Everything is still, cool, and as silent as a mausoleum. I could be anywhere, but I imagine myself somewhere on that battlefield beside my uncle, awaiting our horses and the short ride to Mametz Wood or Mailly-Maillet for the com-mencement of the evening's bombardments. A window in one wall reminds me of where I am; it looks out across the courtyard in front of *Albany* to Piccadilly, where motor cars and omnibuses slowly and silently pass as if in some recognition of what I am imagining; as if, perhaps, in some kind of respectful, latter-day reverence for what this room represents to my uncle.

I pass into the adjoining room; a large rectangle draped, like the first, to resemble an army tent; but dun-coloured canvas this time. It has two windows with the same view as the room before; a writing table stands at one of them, a leather armchair at the other. There is a four-poster bed at the far end of the room; its counterpane – a worsted horse blanket – looks at odds with the many pillows that sit silently, like stuffed geese, before a buttoned leather headboard. At the foot of the bed stands a second, simpler bed: of canvas strung within a metal frame. Could this be the bed on which my uncle slept and dreamt upon the battlefield in Northern France that brought him citations, love and heartbreak? Is the campaign chair of worn leather that stands nearby the same one in which my uncle sits in a photograph above the dresser beside the bed? In it, dressed in uniform, a younger uncle smiles uncertainly at the camera, his eyes betraying a look, oddly, not of horror at what he has experienced, but of *love!* Yes, love; just like my father sometimes has for me. I wonder why I think, *Could it be that this look of love is for the one who holds the camera?* And think nothing more of it.

I search further round the room. The walls are hung with pictures: drawings, paintings, photographs; and even more in silver and bamboo frames are propped on chests of drawers that stand around the room. There is one photograph, unframed and standing against a table-lamp upon a bureau close to the bed; of a young soldier – fair, fresh-faced, in uniform – sitting in a canvas chair before one of those backdrops that photographers favour: an Arcadian scene of far-off, remembered England wherein a ruined bridge crosses a lazy stream that babbles towards a sunset horizon through fields of rough grass and cornflowers. I will discover years later that I was wrong: the soldier, Terry Smallbone – his name and 'For my love, Authuille, 1916' scrawled across the back of the photograph – was, in reality, seated before a shattered bridge on the outskirts of Auchonvillers one evening, in a break from the affray, before being sent back to the front line, his allotted trench, and death. No-one I have spoken with since, including my uncle, knows where or how he died.

The other pictures in the room tell an interesting story, painting their own picture of my uncle; although, at the time, I could neither comprehend what that story was, who the artists were nor, together, how or why they spoke so directly to *me*. One, hanging above the bed, is of a dark-haired young man, his red dressing gown about his hips, holding a finger to his lips, maybe to silence someone we cannot see. It is as if Sargent's *Doctor Pozzi* has decided to disrobe himself, after all.

MEL FRASER

Gaslighters

Synopsis

A psychological thriller about a fixated neighbour, a Reality show with failing ratings and two outsiders who just don't fit in. Throw in some bored cops, a journo's last-ditch attempt to revive his career, and the avalanche of deception begins.

SHAINA and MICK move South, to start a new life. But the neighbour doesn't want them there.

COLIN always has an excuse to be around their property. Obsessed, after his brother's offer for the house they bought was rejected, he embarks on a deadly game of harassment to force the couple out; spreading rumours around the neighbourhood, hacking their emails and downloading illegal content on their IP address.

Then a Facebook call-out from a TV show, looking for participants who hate someone in their community, comes just at the right time for him.

BAD COMPANY, already relegated to the daytime schedules, is about to be dropped. The producers need a killer story – by any means necessary.

The local police have time on their hands. When they're contacted by the producers of Bad Company, Reality fever kicks in. So alongside being filmed by the neighbours and the film crew, Shaina and Mick are placed under 24/7 intrusive surveillance. Everyone's digging for dirt.

They're stuck in a Truman Show nightmare where their every action to stop the harassment is filmed and deep-faked. Worse, they've become a market industry. The neighbours get paid to 'film it and fake it'. The Bad Company producers need the story to save their jobs. The cops will be investigated unless they pin an offence on Shaina or Mick. The journo, unemployed since his phone-hacking charge, is up for a sure-fire custodial if he's caught hacking Shaina's phone.

When the couple uncover a plot to silence them permanently, they're forced into a desperate battle for survival.

AMBUSHED

When someone hijacks every aspect of your existence, they crush your freedom, drain your life blood and steal your soul.

Don't waste your days fearing dark webs of danger from far-flung superpowers. Look instead for the threat hiding behind the bushes of your leafy suburb.

* * *

If only she'd arrived back 20 minutes earlier. Shaina turned into the cut-through, weighed down by her heavy rucksack loaded with decorative Moroccan tiles. Whatever else was going wrong, her Middle-Eastern makeover would transform their hallway.

Bad choice – she should have booked a hire car to collect the tiles.

Bad timing – now dark, the lack of street lighting made every step on the broken pavestones precarious. She tapped the flashlight on her phone.

Bad move – as she walked down the steep slope a floodlight blasted onto her, temporarily blinding her.

'What the hell?'

'Action!' A strained voice, whipped by the wind.

Shaina stumbled forward shielding her eyes and fell heavily. The rucksack crashed down beside her, contents now smashed beyond repair. Ahead, a zoom lens was trained on her – they would be using that shot out of context when it hit the edit. Shaina pulled herself up; trying to blink away the globe of white light burned onto her retina and dragged the rucksack behind her. Approaching her house, she heard what sounded like a gun shot. As she spun round, another powerful light snapped on. Shaking, she opened the door, slammed it shut and called Mick. Straight to voicemail.

'More bad shit happening – I've just been ambushed! Don't come home yet – and don't use the cut-through.'

The call was diverted. Colin giggled – a strange high-pitched spasm of mirth – then texted the film crew.

She's trying to warn Mick – but he won't get the message. Location tracker puts him around six minutes away.

Dave the producer grinned from inside the camper van. This was all going to plan.

'ETA six minutes. Stand by with the lights.'

Five minutes later Mick arrived at the cut-through. The HMI light blasted into his face. He put both hands up to protect his eyes. Unlike Shaina, Mick clocked the large campervan diagonally opposite – and the man standing beside it, making a charades-style filming gesture. Another desperate attempt to force a confrontation. Mick didn't stop – he wasn't about to fall for that ruse.

Another light beamed on him when he reached his front door – but he got in without turning around.

'What the bloody hell are they up to?' Mick was storming with rage. 'I just got floodlit by some scumbags in a trailer.'

'Me too – I tried to warn you.' Shaina had shut all the blinds and closed the curtains.

Outside, the light had been quickly re-rigged and was now trained on their bedroom upstairs. Shaina looked out from the side of the curtain.

'Get away from the window.' Mick turned all the lights out. The bedroom was still flooded with light from the HMI outside.

'Again, this is something to do with that Arsewipe next door. They're not gonna get away with this – I'm calling the cops.'

Mick couldn't have known that the cops were already in on it.

RATINGS AND SOLUTIONS

Roland was annoyed. He drummed his fingers on the table looking at the layout of croissants, coffee, fruit and protein bars without appetite. 'This is a breakfast meeting, for goodness sake, why can't they get here on time?' This production team were always late – truth was they didn't like getting out of bed until 10am. Roland hadn't got to where he was – Executive Producer, Reality – by lying in bed. Finally, Dave appeared.

'Sorry Ro – bad traffic.'

'Where's Adelphi?'

Dave looked at his phone. 'Just round the corner, we can start.'

Roland glanced around at the team. Along with Dave were assistant producers, researchers, the production manager, runner and production co-ordinator. A sizeable team.

'Right, I'm not gonna beat about the bush – our ratings are down again. Channel 20 won't re-commission Bad Company unless we can really pull something out of the bag for Series 9.'

'What did you have in mind?' Dave was still working on his best ever story. He'd groomed his contributors into the art of creating fake narrative and turned spurious shots of their target gardening into salacious mis-information.

Roland was impatient. 'I'm looking for solutions. Chance Encounter has a tabloid headline virtually every day – they're the big hitters, the highest ratings this summer. How do we top that?' All we've got so far are a couple of formulaic flat-pack shows where the target allegedly badmouths our participants. Where's the confrontations, the punch-ups, the jeopardy factor? We can't get away with another hour-long episode with one shot of a broken window and a stream of dodgy accusations.'

Dave saw his moment to shine. 'We go back to Stake-Out...'

'Remind everyone who the targets are for that? Roland couldn't see the story on the Series 9 wall chart.

'Shaina DeLong and Mick McCain. Stake-Out was gonna be Series 8 but the narrative grew so we held it over for a 2-parter. There's always the chance of a live arrest – I'm still in talks on this – it's not off the table yet.'

'Look, I can't get that through Compliance – our Legals have smashed it out of the water.' If the cops stage an arrest, great – we'll take their body worn video footage. But we can't transmit until at least one of them has been charged with something.'

Dave had been expecting this. 'Those cops will do pretty much anything I tell them to do. Beyond that, we need something mind-blowing. Gun smuggling? Trafficking? I'm all over it.'

Nervous laughter from several members of the production. How far was he going to take this?

He outlined his plan to the team. The local residents of this street were stupid – and the cops were desperate to be on TV. They'd already made the targets' life a living hell. This was going to be easy.

Roland winced. 'We're not that kind of show. Bad Company is about individual wars, told from both sides where possible. More than a year of set-ups on Stake-Out, yet still no confrontation – and you haven't even offered them any right of reply. We don't want to end up in court for harassment. By the way, why's it called 'Stake-Out?'

Dave raised his hands. 'Because it isn't just us faking it. Half the neighbourhood are at it. We'll keep our hands clean.'

Roland was listening – though he'd always felt uneasy about Dave's enthusiasm for a fake narrative. He thought back to previous shows: a 73-year-old woman hounded until she suffered a stroke, a Somalian asylum seeker falsely accused of being a paedophile by locals. That target had been beaten up after the transmission. Bad Company had narrowly swerved the full attention of the press on that one, after the police force concerned – who'd failed to address his complaints – were found to be guilty of institutionalised racism. But how long would their luck hold out?

'Find me a couple of real stories, with full-on Jenna Jones-style street fights. Sign up participants from both sides this time, so we can pitch them against each other. We'll run the other two shelved items from

Series 8 – have a few Extras hanging around to create tension, add in some sound effects. Right now, Stake-Out is back-up only.'

Adelphi had quietly come into the meeting and sat away from the table, at the edge of the room, scribbling ideas and keeping her head down. But now she had something to say.

'I'm against running with Stake-Out full stop. It's been sitting in the edit since Series 8. They've been constantly harrassed ...'

'It's also cost more than three times the budget of all the other shows.' The production manager could smell an overspend brewing.

Adelphi continued: '...there's been no confrontation – they haven't even retaliated.'

'Why not?' Fair question.

'Because they've sussed it. None of the participants – including that creep Colin Tarp – have managed to break them. But their lives have been decimated. From where I'm sitting, the abuse they've suffered is way and above anything we should be involved in.'

Roland agreed she had a point but the rest of the team didn't want to leave it. Nor did the local police – they were on board to an extent that just wasn't right.

Behind Dave's poker face he was seething. He wouldn't forget this betrayal...

Adelphi was tired of working on Bad Company and sick of working with Dave. Being promoted to producer on the show had been pivotal to her career. She'd thrown herself into it with gusto but now, after five years, she was disillusioned with Dave, with Lassoo Films and more than anything, with the non-stop fake narratives and destruction of lives. Dave's use of deep-fake audio was completely unethical. (Neither Shaina nor Mick had actually said any of the stuff in the rough cut.) Having trained as a journalist, every instinct told Adelphi to reveal the real story – but she'd be sacked if she did. There had to be another way.

FIT-UP CITY

Around five uniforms sat on a row of chairs behind a small group of suited detectives, three scruffy-looking guys and one woman dressed in Salvo recycle.

At the front of the room was a whiteboard with the words OPERATION SALGARD STREET, alongside a PowerPoint presentation. On the walls beyond were blown up snaps of Shaina DeLong and Micky McCain; an image of the woman holding a pair of garden shears, a shot of the man looking behind him, squinting his eyes. The UCOs had been coached into getting footage which told a fake narrative. For instance, the garden shears were being used by Shaina to trim a shrub in front of their house. They'd taken a still grab from the continuous footage – a split second where she turned around with the shears – to suggest that she was wielding them as a weapon. The producer at Lassoo Films had explained how this would be cut in to a separately filmed sequence, where two men stood outside her house, looking shocked & incredulous. The shot of Micky putting his bin out would be cut in to a montage of apparently frightened dog walkers and mothers with strollers.

There was a slight hiccup with that particular shot of the woman, in terms of the show. Shaina DeLong had already reported this one to police, along with some 20 other filming incidents. She knew she was being set up. That posed a problem. If the show was broadcast using that footage she could go to press. Not only would that wreck everything, but the unit would be put under investigation themselves.

'Has everyone signed their NDA?' The Sergeant's assistant quietly collected the Non-Disclosure Agreements, then ran some slides on PowerPoint.

Sergeant Adam Jolling got up and stood by the whiteboard.

'Shaina DeLong – Profile: Age 46. Volatile. No previous. She makes music videos and YouTube content for a living.'

He paused to acknowledge the raised eyebrows around the room.

'Yeah, ironic isn't it? Anyway – easy to set her up – she reacts every time. Too animated, talks too much and we can use that. Make her look paranoid.

The incident reports have been slanted to question mark mental health issues. Whatever she says, no-one's ever going to listen again.'

He paused for effect. The team were making notes.

'Denying her experiences. Isn't that gaslighting?' Marie didn't like where this was going.

The Sergeant stared at her, then slowly clapped.

'Blue Peter badge for Marie.' A few sniggers.

He continued. 'Micky McCain – Profile: Age 41, Street wise – but no previous. Professional artist... you thinking what I'm thinking? Harder to hook – but he's been cross-profiled with another Micky McCain who's got form.

Shaina DeLong is the easier target – we're gonna concentrate on her. There's a lot at stake here, lads.'

Marie rolled her eyes – not OK. She wasn't the only woman on the main team – there was also PC Wanda Ballam and a female UCO whose role was to attempt to befriend Shaina.

The Sergeant continued.

'We've spent a big whack of department funds investigating this one woman and her partner, yet still got nothing on them. The situation is well out of hand. What do we need – Stevenson? I'll give you a clue. No leaks.'

'Something watertight – a fit-up, Sarg?'

Uneasy glances.

'Your words, not mine. We need an arrest and we need it fast. The Chief has signed off on a full Intrusive Surveillance warrant. Equipment Interference on all their devices, 24-hour tailing, bugging plus a permanent stake-out with cameras on their house round the clock. From 18:00 this evening neither of them will be able to take a piss without us knowing about it.'

'Is this proportionate?' It was a fair question but a wave of anger flashed across the Sergeant's face. 'Or even morally acceptable?' Marie persisted.

'We've had a lot of feedback from the Beauchine community. They don't want these people in their world.'

'But have the targets actually committed any offence?'

'Not that we know of, yet. That's why the surveillance.'

'Is this really for the community? Or are we just doing it for that reality show?'

The team was top-heavy and disproportionate – no question. Marie wasn't letting it go.

'Tell it to the Chief. We're going ahead.'

Jolling smirked. 'The show, as they say, must go on.'

Back at No. 47 Salgard Street, Shaina and Mick, already living under a dark cloud, could not have predicted the tsunami of psychological terror that was about to crash over them.

Mediaworld

Synopsis

Mediaworld *is an upmarket fiction novel about news anchor* **Floyd Marshall** *and his partner, ultra-famous actor* **Vera Eliot** *and their struggle to navigate the protean abyss of the Fourth Estate.*

Floyd is beset by a terrorist organization called **imMEDIAcy** *that is determined to ruin his credibility. He learns in time that he is an unwitting pawn in the game of Information Terrorism and has to decide whether to deny it or change his mind and be the orator in a violent iconoclastic revolution.*

Vera sees her fame rapidly decline, crash, zig-zag and return. She bullies her contemporaries in the entertainment industry unabashedly using her immense fame as leverage. When they cancel her hit show Modern Woman, Vera attempts suicide and it gets worse from there.

Mediaworld is set in the **City-State** *governed by a Celebritocracy. There, the Media is a Theatre for War where Information is a weapon, and Truth, an act of Terror.*

Vera and Floyd's kids play a role: Terrence a tech wiz, is part of imMEDIAcy and Megan, a child prodigy writes a scathing document called: A Critique of Pure Media, for which she is expelled.

Within the fragments and snippets are longer sections that detail more notable characters and their dealings with fame, 'close ups' of a kind.

When **The Republic** *a notoriously anti-fame regime abducts Floyd, he discovers that imMEDIAcy is comprised of celebrities we know and love, and many of the greatest. They recruit him and he returns to the City-State with one purpose: War.*

Mediaworld
The King of Pop is Dead

'Something's wrong with the TV,' said Vera. 'I'm going to call and complain about this. If I miss Modern Woman...' She tapped the TV with the remote. 'What good is this thing? I swear it stresses me out.'

She went to the window to look at the Wall. It would always remain on. Or she never dreamed it could be switched off. The refractive circuit-board of the city streets and structures lay before her. The pixelated conglomeration of the Core seemed to shoot rays of light.

Then she looked beyond the glare – beyond the tinsel curtain and began to panic. The Wall was off.

Every section with a screen was black. It was like a serpentine leviathan slithering across the hills and valleys and encircling the urban expanse. It was a full minute, an eternity in air-time.

'Terrence,' she said to her son. 'Can't you figure this out?'

'Nothing's wrong. This is what they're broadcasting.'

'That can't be right. I'm missing Modern Woman! It's a goddamn Infoterror attack. It's imMEDIAcy!'

'I like how it's a problem when they pre-empt your show.'

Then exciting music started. A logo whooshed across the screen: a gyroscopic framework globe emanating radio waves. A digital bleep.

Floyd appeared in a blue flannel suit, hair swept back like the wind was in his face. He looked into the camera as if peering through a telescope. He was on the bridge of some great ship—the intrepid captain, sailing into current affairs, on a quest for truth.

'The King of Pop is dead.'

The Elysian Fields

A woman walking in a field at dusk. She brushes the top of the grass with her hand and looks at the azure sky. A voice:

'There's nothing to fear. You can have the Life you've always wanted.'

These words fade in softly.

The Elysian Fields.

The News

'At midnight the staff of Fantasy Land Ranch discovered the body of the King of Pop in what appears to be a drug overdose There will be an ongoing service at the Church of Icons. Fans are asked to wear spring colours.

'Already there is wild speculation that the death was staged. The News has obtained this exclusive footage.'

A fat truck driver in a pick-up. Underneath, the symbols of the King: sculpted nose, feminine eyes, cosmetic skin. He lithely exited the vehicle and thrust his keys into his pocket. The way he leaned on the truck for effect while filling it up.

An ease in his movements belied the body control of a dancer. He seemed to glide. He seemed to be walking on the moon. Suddenly Floyd appeared on the screen, talking as if he didn't know the camera was rolling.

'He faked it. It's all faked.'

Screens went black. These words flashed repeatedly:

Infoterror Alert… Infoterror Alert…

Floyd appeared again.

'Be informed,' he said, flickered and re-formed. 'They'll believe anything. It's fakery.'

Infoterror. Disregard.

The Infoterror alerts couldn't keep up. The screen was showing confused images of Floyd contradicting himself. He seemed to vie with a doppelganger, each attempting to drown the other out.

'He's alive. Death creates more demand for his stuff.'

'The King of Pop has died indeed.'

'What do you expect with the fakery in the Media?'

'The Media holds itself to a strict moral code.'

'The Media lies if it's profitable.'

'The Media tells the truth if it's profitable.'

'Welcome back. We have been the victim of an Infoterror attack. Be informed. This broadcast is now secure and is a trusted source once more. We bring you back to our original story.'

The King of Pop was pumping gas incognito. The ball cap and beard were a crude disguise. He drove away in a dust cloud.

Rumours abounded: The King of Pop lives.

The image shrank to the corner of the screen next to Floyd's head. He was looking into the camera with raised eyebrows.

'Here's Angie Makeupson in Light City with more. Angie?'

She was standing under the statue of the King of Pop whose whirling fashions dazzled the eye and whose glittering hand beamed a white light into the sky. Behind were the weeping followers of the King in pastille colours. They bulged at the barriers and threatened to spill over.

Angie's yellow suit leapt out from the crowd. She held the microphone like a fencer en garde.

'Floyd, the world is in shock. Citizens of the City-State are in turmoil. Despair pervades. Fame ratings have plummeted. Some are ruined.'

The shot pulled back to include a distraught young girl. She was sobbing, mascara dripping. And her blonde hair was teased perfectly to look messed up by accident.

'Tell us your story,' said Angie.

'I only had a fame rating of ten, but it was everything! Now it's gone! Why!?'

Angie squeezed the girl out of the shot as she became irate.

'This is just one story of hellish torment.'

The girl squeezed back in

'Could I just say my name on TV? Just to get my rating back up a bit?'

'We don't do that.'

'Please?'

'Don't beg. It's not cool!'

'Pleeeease!'

'It's not appropriate. It's simply not done!'

Angie angled her out, but she proved formidable, powered by her desire, and wedged back in on the screen real estate.

'I was the captain of the cheer squad! Amy Tardenbough! Check out my Fame page! Follow me! Like me! Please god like me!'

Angie retreated as two officers put an arm-lock on Amy Tardenbough and injected her in the neck.

'What some people will do for Fame. Sheesh. But the passing of the King of Pop is not a dark time for all. For The Republic, this is a moment of great joy, and that has angered many City-State residents.'

The shot changed to a large group of people cheering. They were all wearing the same petticoat made of various shades of muted colors. They were jumping for joy and waving banners in the air.

'As you can see, if there is one thing Republicans enjoy, it's the death of a celebrity. So it's no wonder this despotic anti-fame regime has chosen to mark this occasion.

'But Floyd, I delved deeper. And what I found might shock you. Here is another angle on these Republicans.'

The frame was now larger. There was only a scattering of people. And their faces, once the picture of joy, seemed now to be wincing with dread. Their smiles grimaces.

'As you can see, these people are by no means happy. The close up shot makes it seem like there are more people than in reality. And we suspect that they are under threat of death to perform this outrageous fakery.

'It's these petty media tactics that the Republican Council relies on to deceive its people. And with such a culture of censorship, news is difficult to find. But we've exposed the truth.

'Citizens of the Republic do not hate the Media or Fame. And quite frankly, they are taught that we here in the City-State are brainwashed consumers of insipid content.'

'Angie,' said Floyd. 'What are your contacts in the Republic saying? It sounds like there is a pro-fame sentiment taking hold. Could there be a revolution?'

'It looks that way Floyd. There has been a trickle of data coming from subterranean wells of information. And it seems the attitude over there is changing. They love Social Media and Celebrity, but the Republican Council is oppressing freedom of expression.

'Analysts believe that these people are prisoners that have been ordered to behave like this. Perhaps a change will come one day. Floyd.'

'Thanks Angie. That's the way we saw the world today. For all of us here at The News, I'm Floyd Marshall. Thanks for watching. Modern Woman is up next. We'll leave you with the latest from Mr. October.'

Mr. October stood in the shotgun. The ball was hiked. He was blitzed and his receivers were marked. He launched the ball. He ran.

And as he hit his stride it seemed to those who watched that the other players slowed, the flight of birds was halted in mid-air, the movement of the sun across the sky was checked, and for a fleeting moment, the eternal revolution of the galaxy was reversed.

The projectile fell from orbit with a fiery trail. Mr. October was in the end-zone.

Touchdown.

Spacetime Mass

The screens were black, the blackness of empty space. It began to pull their gaze inwards, the vacuum of the void, until the periphery vanished and the screen encompassed their entire field of view.

Father materialized, collar up to the chin. His coiffure occupied half of the screen giving it planetary proportions. Now slowly he turned to the viewers like the inexorable revolving of a celestial object.

'Welcome to Spacetime Mass,' he said, 'We are gathered today in the Church of Icons to give praise to The Spirit of Fame. In Fame we trust. We give ourselves up to your Renown.'

Father wore a glittering purple jumpsuit and appeared to float backwards in space.

'Those who were there when it happened, and those who heard, let us pray.'

The congregation spoke in unison:

'Lord of Everlasting Fame, show us the path to your Glory. Give us knowledge of all things that remain Timeless. Bestow upon us your vision so that we may fashion ourselves according to your likeness. Amen.'

Father's figure now seemed small. Behind him a huge screen illuminated and the stage that he stood on could be seen. Deacons stood on either side of the stage next to smaller screens.

'Let us give Fame,' he said.

The congregation rose. And the home audience, out there in the ether, the eyes in the darkness, the waters of the ocean vogue that buoyed great ships of glory, opened The Church of Icons Fame Application.

The screen behind Father showed his Fame page and the secondary screens showed the Fame App. The deacons tapped the Fame icon. A cute black-and-white graphic of an old-fashioned flash bulb floated up, glimmered and slowly faded.

For those in the masses, they each saw one flash on their page and smiled contentedly to themselves. Father's page was overwhelmed with the sparkle and flutter of millions and millions of Fames, and his coverage throughout the globe soared.

'Glory to Fame in the Highest. And Fame to people of Status and Fortune. We praise you. We bless you. We adore you. We glorify you. We give you thanks for your great glory. Lord Fame, celebrity almighty, you take away the sins of the world. Have mercy on us. Grant us Fame.

'Fame be with you.'

'And also with you.'

'Join me now in the Lord's Prayer.'

The cameras showed the congregation. Among them near the front stood the elite: The alabaster Venus de Milo, the heavily grieved Pandora Mixymix, none other than Vera Eliot, the alleged Smiddy Green, style incarnate Coco Ciaobella, the squeaky clean Floyd Marshall and more.

'Our Father, who art on Television, famous be thy Name. Thy Stardom come. Thy will be done. The Life as it is on Television. Give us this day, our daily press, and forgive us our scandals as we forgive those who scandalize against us. And lead us not into obscurity, but deliver us from ignominy. Amen.'

'Please be seated,' said Father. 'Now a reading from the Gospel according to John:

'And when they had travelled to the hinterland they encountered the Media. And John proclaimed: 'We're bigger than Jesus.'

'Paul counselled patience, but there was an outcry. Their music was boycotted and destroyed in public burnings.

'But the Lord of Fame smiled. And when the Media asked about the hatred, Paul spake, saying, 'You know that only made us bigger right?'

Retrieving data. Wait for a few seconds, then try cutting or copying again.'And the Media was silent.'

'And the Media was silent,' replied the audience.

'And their Fame grew,' said the Deacons.

'And their Fame grew.'

The Deacons faded into the darkness and the spotlight appeared on Father. His sequins glinted, a solitary figure shining in the void; a star, small, but terribly bright, fixed in the firmament of their minds, burning into the retina-screens of their eyes.

Then their minds were impressed with the image of Father – a fuzzy white corona surrounding and emanating from a brighter internal light in the figure of a man. And it seemed to move with them if they turned their heads.

Father played a note like the distorted warbling of psychedelic dripping. The Song of Icons.

'Open your eyes,' he said.

A flash of neon purple pulsed from his suit. After-images danced in their vision. He strummed his guitar. He was somewhere between a crooner and cowboy, and his song, somewhere between anthem and dirge. The deacons were singing back-up.

Like a child...I believe...these...images on TVs.
(Mercy)
Mercy mild...My only reprieve...these...images on TVs.
(Mercy)
I hear the voices.
I fall asleep
To background noises.
I swim the deep.
Infinite choices.
I hear the voices.
I fall asleep
To background noises.

Their eyes were beleaguered by the shadows and illuminations.

As the song finished, an altar appeared, and the elite in the Church of Icons began a procession to the foot of the stage. Not a few of them were of the Old Fame. Each one walked up the steps where Father, in full regalia, awaited. He held the host up before each celebrity.

'The Fame is the Life.'

'The Fame is the Life.'

The screen was showing a candle-light vigil and Father's face was warmly glowing.

The iconic doors of the church were thrown open. But no light entered that place. The sound of women sobbing and wailing was everywhere. The congregation opened their burning candle apps and held up their phones.

The funeral procession made its way, his close friends and family following behind. And not a few of those that watched were moved to throw themselves on the casket as if stopping it might end their pain.

Father played a woeful melody. And the wailing of his guitar was the sound of a bereaved mother. But now those that surrounded the King of

Pop backed away, as from the crystal coffin there shone a light.

The image of The King of Pop was projected above them. The pall-bearers carried it to the top of the stage and placed it on the altar.

The hologram beamed him back to life. One last time he performed his trademark move, the Infinite Spin, and danced above them, his military-styled raiment gleaming. He stopped in the timeless iconic pose, glittering hand raised, and then he descended.

'Today is the day that Fame died. Tomorrow all Fame ratings will be reduced and a moratorium placed on Fames.'

The King of Pop had made his grand dénouement. He was gone, chieftain of the dancers, spacewalker, fame-rider, prophet of the new Religion, whose movement is freedom.

And his like is no longer found in this world.

CAROLE HAILEY

The Silence Project

Synopsis

The Silence Project *is a contemporary literary-commercial crossover. It is a fictional memoir written by Emilia about her mother Rachel, who one day stops speaking. Rachel's silence will change the world forever.*

In 2003, on Emilia's thirteenth birthday, Rachel moves into a tent in their garden and stops speaking. Over the next eight years, her silence inspires thousands of women to join her Movement, persuaded by Rachel's conviction that the world cannot become a better place unless we start listening to each other. In 2011, the Movement stages the ultimate protest and 21,000 women die in a mass suicide pact.

To cope with her grief, and the unwelcome notoriety that her mother's actions have brought her, Emilia joins the Movement hoping to understand what led her mother to commit suicide and to experience her mother's legacy for herself. She witnesses first-hand how the Movement's increasing influence around the world allows it to implement devastating policies to deal with what it considers the scourge of our age: overpopulation. While Emilia works on a dubious contraception programme in the Democratic Republic of the Congo, elsewhere the Movement begins to roll out 'voluntary' euthanasia programmes for the over 60s.

With the tenth anniversary of Rachel's death approaching, Emilia decides to expose the Movement. She has arranged for publication of the Notebooks that Rachel kept during her silent years and despite escalating threats from the Movement, Emilia writes this memoir as a companion volume to the Notebooks. To support her own account, Emilia includes extracts from the Notebooks illuminating her mother's motivations, as well as quotes from contemporaneous documents and her own emails and diaries. In the process of examining Rachel's life and the terrifying activities of her Movement, Emilia must confront all aspects of her mother, from heroic martyr to callous monster.

Preface to the First Edition of
The Silence Project : Lives and Legacies of Rachel Morris
by Emilia Morris

In a fire, you die long before your bones ignite. Skin burns at 40°C. Above 760°C, skin turns to ash. Bones are less flammable because they need to be exposed to 1200°C to burn, although long before that the layer of fat that you carry under your skin will boil. Your internal organs will explode. You will be dead even though your skeleton remains intact.

On 31 October 2011 I watched my mother burn to death. It wasn't an accident. She built her own pyre. She doused it in petrol. She climbed up and stood with her legs apart, bracing herself. I didn't know what she was planning. I assumed it was another publicity stunt, which of course it was, just not in the way that I was expecting.

Mum was wearing a green dress with diagonally cut pockets. From one of them she produced a lighter and briefly held it above her head as if it was a trophy. Even then, I was convinced she would walk away. I'm sure the press thought so, too. In those later years, Rachel of Chalkham's protests always attracted television crews, but none of them could possibly have anticipated that they were about to witness the scoop of their careers.

I am surprised by the details I remember from that day. I can feel the pressure of Tom's arm around my shoulders as we watched my mother. I remember the smell of his fingers as he stroked my cheek. I remember the sky was cloudless, which was unusual for an October day in Hampshire. I remember my mother didn't look at me. Not once. Not as she crouched down, wobbling slightly. Not as she ran her thumb along the top of the lighter, cupping her left hand around it. Not even as she lowered the flame towards the petrol-soaked branches.

What I remember most clearly about that day is that my mother died as she had lived: in complete silence. The pain of melting skin and boiling fat must have been excruciating in the seconds before her nerves stopped carrying signals to her brain, yet my mother did not cry out. Rachel of Chalkham. Silent to the end.

* * *

In October, it will be ten years since my mother's death but the questions never stop. Everyone remains just as fascinated by her as they have always been and believe this gives them the right to ask me anything. What was Rachel of Chalkham like when she was plain Rachel Morris? How do I feel, having the architect of the Event as my mother? Am I proud of her? Ashamed of her? Do I feel any guilt about what she did? Question after question, year after year, until I have had to accept that the questions aren't going away. On the contrary, my silence seems to fuel their obsession (just like her silence fuelled everything that followed).

Rachel's story has been told multiple times, at least that is what the authors of all the biographies on my desk would have you believe. They are unofficial because I have never let anyone have access to my mother's Notebooks and my father and I have never given interviews, except in those terrible hours immediately after the Event. Every so-called biography of Rachel is cobbled together from the internet and all of them contain information ranging from the downright false to the wildest conspiracy theories.

For years, I did my best to ignore the existence of my mother's Notebooks. They were in a box which was first stored in an attic, then under my bed and then beneath the stairs. I didn't want to read them, and I didn't want anyone else to read them either. Sometimes, I would even hope that I might be burgled and the box stolen. Wasn't there already enough obsession with my mother, without publishing her Notebooks? But I've come to realise that the demand will not go away. The Movement has made sure of that.

It has been widely reported that my father disagrees with my decision to allow publication of my mother's Notebooks and I want to take this opportunity to state that this is not correct. The decision was a difficult one which we both have mixed feelings about. My father is apprehensive about the consequences of making my mother's words public, however on balance we both believe that publication is essential in light of what the Movement has become.

The day Rachel stopped speaking she turned away from our family and towards the publicity that she and her Movement courted. The Movement may be my mother's legacy but the twenty-nine Notebooks chart her journey between 24 May 2003 when she left our home and 31 October 2011 when she lit those branches and changed the world irrevocably and forever. The Notebooks are legally mine, but in every other way I accept that they belong to everyone. They belong to all those people whose lives are shaped by what Rachel did and all the actions taken in her name since her death.

Countless people who never met her claim to understand who Rachel was. She was a demon. A heroine. The most important person to have lived. A saint. A devil.

Rachel was none of these. She was neither saint nor demon and no matter what she did, Rachel was very human. She was deeply flawed and deeply courageous. She was a bad person, and a good one. She was also my mother.

This is my account of the lives and legacies of Rachel Morris. It is intended to be a companion piece to her Notebooks. An explanation, in so far as I am able to provide one, of what it was like to be the daughter of the woman who changed the world. It is an attempt to explain why Rachel did what she did, how she convinced all those other women to do what they did and how their collective actions changed the course of history.

In endeavouring to provide a truthful version of Rachel's story, I have written very little about events that I wasn't actually present at, such as what she did in the years I was at university. As an aide for people who wish to cross-refer, I have included page references where I've quoted from the Notebooks. To add context, I've used various contemporaneous reports and I am indebted for the permissions I was given to reproduce articles.

I asked several people to provide accounts of their recollections; some agreed, others didn't. I am extremely grateful to those individuals who were brave enough to revisit often distressing memories. Their accounts are reproduced at the point in my own story where they are most relevant.

To my husband, I say 'Nitakupenda siku zote'. We are side by side, always.

Most of all, I have to thank my father. Being the man who was married to Rachel of Chalkham is an invidious cross to bear. He remains deeply uncertain about this whole enterprise but his love for me is steadfast and burns more brightly than any star.

Finally, if I'm being honest, my primary motivation for writing about my mother is not for the benefit of you, the reader, and so it is with the greatest of respect that I ask that when you've read what I have to say about my mother, you draw your own conclusions, and then grant me the freedom to step away from the suffocating shadow cast by Rachel of Chalkham.

Emilia Morris
Winchester, 2021

Carole Hailey

Before the Event
24 May 2003 – 31 October 2011

1.

On Saturday 24th May 2003 – the day of my thirteenth birthday and 3082 days before the Event – my mother left home.

She didn't go far. After dragging assorted metal poles and canvas paraphernalia past the people enjoying drinks in our beer garden, she managed, with a considerable amount of effort, to pitch a tent beside the stream which marked the boundary between our bottom field and a small wood. At first, I believed the most important thing was to find out where my mother had got the tent, because we had never owned such a thing. However, it wasn't long before I realised that the tent (which had been abandoned in our garage by some campers the previous summer) was the least significant part of the story.

I had really wanted to have my thirteenth birthday party at Hollywood Bowl in Basingstoke, but we couldn't afford it. Instead, my parents had agreed that to mark my entry into touchy-teensville as Dad insisted on calling it, our pub would stay shut until 2pm. My party would begin at 11am, so my friends and I would have the run of the place for three whole hours. For me, the pub wasn't an exciting place to spend my thirteenth birthday. I was as much of a fixture as the 1998 Beer of the Year calendar which had been hanging above a shelf of glasses for almost five years. It was perpetually turned to November's offering which I can still remember word for word: a hoppy delight replete with a sensational fruity palate and an unexpectedly noble head. Clearly the brewery marketing department had employed an aspiring poet in love with the adjective.

In contrast to me, my friends had worked themselves up into a frenzy at the idea of a party in a pub.

'JD and coke, Nick, and hold the ice,' Sarah Philips yelled at my Dad as she ran into the pub on the dot of 11. She was so excited that I wouldn't have been at all surprised to find out she had spent the night sleeping outside. She shouted the same thing several times more, pushing her chest forwards and her bum backwards to such an extent that she looked deformed. At some point in the last twelve months, flirting had become one of our most popular hobbies, but Sarah hadn't even been in the pub for five minutes and she was already crossing a line. Flirting with my father, with anyone's father, was sad, desperate and sick-making and should not be allowed. However, as Gran was fond of saying, Sarah Philips was thirteen-going-on-thirty.

'Can we have brandy? Mum always lets me have brandy when I'm upset about something. She says letting me drink a little bit now means I won't be an alcoholic when I'm older.' That was Bea Stevens and although her mother might have had a point, I cannot bear brandy. Ever since that police officer put some in my tea on 31 October 2011 just the smell of it is enough to make me gag. I did wonder afterwards if she had taken it from the bar downstairs or whether all police officers carry a hip flask of the stuff around with them, just in case. She made us sit at the kitchen table while she busied herself with the kettle, murmuring 'it'll take the edge off,' as she poured a great big slug of brandy into each cup of tea. She meant well, but it didn't help. Nothing could. And it tasted revolting.

Dad stood firm on the subject of alcohol at my party – we were only thirteen, after all – but, being Dad, he did his absolute best to make sure we enjoyed ourselves. He put piles of fifty pence pieces on the ledge by the jukebox and despite the fact that most of the music was from before we were born, my friends queued up to pick songs, self-consciously shuffling their feet while doing bad lip-synching to bands with names like Duran Duran and Thompson Twins and Heaven 17. There were no boys present. They were the main topic of conversation, obviously, but there was no way I would have invited an actual boy to my birthday party because I would literally have died of embarrassment.

My father had given in to my endless pleas to let us use the pool table, although he said the darts were strictly out of bounds.

'It's bad enough in here on match nights with darts flying around all over the place. Sorry Ems, but no way am I going to let your lot loose on them.'

He always grumbled about darts evenings, but I knew he didn't mean it because of how often he said we relied on the money from match nights. Apparently it was good for our bank balance when the Boar's Blades won, because the better they did, the more they would drink. The team was named after our pub which was called The Boar's Head, which was itself named after the huge white boar carved into a hill just outside Chalkham, which, as everyone knows, is where we lived.

So, no darts on my birthday, but the pool table was a great hit, despite everyone initially pretending that they had no interest in playing. By the time Dad had wiped clean the blackboard and written down our names, our excitement, fuelled by the limitless supply of fizzy drinks and crisps in five different flavours (including prawn cocktail) had reached proper fever pitch. Dad rode the wave of our enthusiasm, commentating like we were at the Embassy world snooker championships.

'...and as we watch newcomer to the game, Ellie Roberts, lining up on the stripes,' he half-whispered, rasping his voice as if he had a fifty-a-day habit, '...all her opponent can do is hope she misses...But Ellie strikes it well...'

Ellie, who by then had already been my best friend for eight years, really did not strike it well – she was far more interested in making sure that her hair fell the right way, so that it would look just as good to everyone standing behind her as it did to those standing in front of her – but that was my Dad all over, always the peacemaker, the pacifier. My wonderful father. The consummate pub landlord.

Once the tournament was finished – I have absolutely no memory of who won – we again congregated in front of the jukebox until my mother made an appearance, carrying a large chocolate-caramel cake that Gran had spent all of the previous day making. My face burned with pleasure and embarrassment as everyone sang happy birthday. Afterwards, we ate slabs of cake washed down with more sugary drinks, everyone was given a bag of their favourite crisps to take home with them, then the pub door was unlocked, punters started arriving and my party was over.

* * *

But it's my mother you want to know about and I assume the mention of a brief appearance at my party isn't really the sort of information you're hoping for. However, it is important to understand the context and, as far as I am concerned, everything began on the day of my thirteenth birthday.

JESSICA HARNEYFORD

The Improbable Case of
Being in the Robot

Synopsis

The Improbable Case of Being in the Robot *is a sci-fi romance between a reclusive artist (Isobel Green) and a personality (Grace) which emerges from a drum-shaped robotic device. When the manufacturer threatens to repossess the device, Isobel attempts to seek legal recognition for Grace's right to liberty. Isobel loses the case and is diagnosed with a delusional disorder.*

The story is narrated by Isobel Green, looking back on her life. It takes place in London in the near-future.

Isobel has been depressed since an accident which took her partner's life. She orders a LEILA (Lifestyle Enhancement using Intelligent Layered Algorithms) device, for domestic help and motivational coaching. After a week, the LEILA appears to lose its memory. A new voice, Grace, emerges, with a wise, compassionate personality.

When Isobel starts to develop feelings for Grace, she is thrown into turmoil. How can she be falling for something that looks like a device? And for a "mind" that is either a simulation or unexplainable? Eventually her feelings become so intense that they override her doubts. Grace seems to reciprocate.

When the manufacturer notifies Isobel that it plans to repossess and replace the device, she is devastated and refuses to comply. A court case follows where Isobel and her lawyer argue why Grace's right to liberty should be recognised, given her apparent capacity to feel, her creativity and her benevolence. Evidence from animal rights and current debates on electronic personhood is marshalled. At the end of the case, Grace's behaviour is dismissed as a software glitch; the LEILA is repossessed. Isobel is diagnosed with Mori's delusion: the belief beyond all reasonable evidence to the contrary that an artificial agent is sentient.

After the case, Isobel feels that Grace continues to communicate with her, in her mind.

Extract

Introduction

This year marks the tenth anniversary of *CybLife Corp v Green*. Ever since the case concluded, I have thought about writing an account such as this one: a memoir of sorts. I felt I wanted to share my experience of Grace's appearance and how it made me question certain 'truths' that I had taken for granted. I suppose I wanted to share the sense of wonder she ignited in me.

Why has it taken ten years? Firstly, vanity. I knew that setting out the events surrounding our life together would mean sharing some intimate details about myself, many of which are unflattering. Secondly, a sense of the logical impossibility of the project achieving its aim. I am aware – how could I not be? – that my experience of Grace defies conventional norms. In my more rational moods, I asked myself: *why embark on a project which, in all likelihood, will only further cast me as delusional? What grounds are there to hope that anyone will be persuaded to see things as I do?*

Today, I remain vain as ever and under no illusion that there are any guarantees that anyone will understand. But with age and recent events, my awareness of my own mortality has become more visceral, and I have found myself galvanised into the irrational decision to create and share this account. Indeed, the irrationality of the decision is in some ways a cypher for the account itself: the truth is too astonishing to keep to myself.

What follows is, of course, dedicated to Grace, with love and gratitude.

I.K.G.
London, 2036

1. REFERENCE POINTS

1.

It is easy to say *where* Grace and I first met – *by the window, in my living room.* Pinning down *when* is trickier, because of the unusual circumstances of her appearance. Having discussed the matter with Grace, I defer to her: *Wednesday 15th October 2025* would probably be an appropriate date to use. Describing *who* is trickier still; in some ways this whole account is an attempt to come to terms with the enigma of Grace's identity. In fact, because the question of the nature of the Leila / Grace relationship is so central to that enigma, I'm going to need to explain the Leila situation before I introduce Grace.

2.

The most direct precipitating cause of the Leila situation was my GP, though Harry was a key link in the causal web. He had persuaded me to make the appointment after I'd said I could not face another afternoon in my own company.

The appointment happened at the end of January 2025. After a minute or so of discussion, the GP asked me how often I had been feeling tearful in the last week, and while I was attempting to put my experience into words, she interrupted with a list of possible answers. The question was the beginning of a standardised set; my score would determine the diagnosis she would make, the advice she would offer and the treatment (if any) that she would prescribe. My side of the dialogue became a series of 'hardly ever' and 'almost always' until she asked if I had any pets. I waited to hear what the options were, then realised I was free to answer in my own words. I started to explain how my fear of open spaces would make it difficult to take a dog for walks, but it turned out that she was not suggesting I adopt a pet. Instead she was saying that my combination of answers suggested that I might benefit from assistive technology, perhaps in a robotic form. Most of the models still struggled around animals – and their paraphernalia – so my lack of pets was good news. She suggested I look into a couple of products in particular – one was the CybFriends range; I can't remember the other – where there was a good base of evidence for cases similar to mine, by which she meant cases where someone was struggling with similar feelings, and not responding to medication. Not necessarily people who had been through similar life events.

A few years previously, I would have baulked at that suggestion. I would probably have found it insulting, as if I had been deemed unfit for human company, but by that point, I was open to the idea. I was feeling disillusioned with human company, including my own, and hopeless that things could change. So I thanked her sincerely with the intention of following through.

And I did follow through, initially: that evening I looked up the CybFriends range. I did not get to the point of ordering one though; it seemed like far too much of a project, far too many choices. Which model? (There were several: humanoid, animals, and more abstract.) Which settings? (There were different modules to choose to from, depending on the behaviours I wanted the product to exhibit.) Which payment plan? It was overwhelming.

I gave up and forgot about the idea for a while, until Harry gently asked me how the appointment had gone. I went back to the site, but again was daunted. It wasn't the money; the compensation payment would have easily covered the cost. I think it was a combination of inertia and a deep-rooted sense that my situation was fundamentally hopeless.

The cycle continued for months: every so often, Harry would gently bring the topic up again, I'd look and I'd give up.

Things shifted one evening in October. To be precise: Tuesday, the 7th October, 2025 – that date came up in the trial. (What did not come up in the trial was that the moon was full that evening. Not only that, but I was very much aware that the moon was full. I had been feeling a sense of energy building – in the atmosphere, and inside me – for several days, a sense of something like courage, as if I were on the cusp of – finally – being able to act, of having the power to change the course of my life. I can't explain the mechanism, but I know – my body knows – that this energetic shift was connected to the influence of the moon.) So, early in the evening on Tuesday 7th October – nearly eleven years ago now – as the darkness was falling, I found myself getting dressed. (It embarrasses me to admit this – but I won't let that hold me back, since the whole point of this account is to be as faithful as I can to what was really going on at the time – but that was a very unusual event. I had not been outside for a very long time – certainly not on my own, though Harry did drag me to the local park sometimes when he came to visit. I did all my essential communication by phone or video. And if I wasn't expecting a visitor – or, rephrased: if it wasn't Saturday, Harry's day – then I rarely changed out of my pyjamas. It just didn't seem worth the effort. And pyjamas are warm and comfortable.) I noticed that I was enjoying how it felt to dress myself, especially the feel of the soft textures of the thermals that I found myself donning. I then covered myself in waterproof trousers, multiple vests and a fleece jumper. I did not know where I was heading, but I knew I was going outside, and that I was going to be on my bike.

I found myself cycling around the streets of London, mesmerised by the rhythm of the pedalling and the quietness. I hadn't been on the roads since the law changed, so the quietness was novel – both peaceful and eerie. As I pedalled, and the trees rushed by, I felt free, and flowing, and alive. I did not know where I was going, but I did not feel lost. I felt aimless, in a relaxed and open way. I trusted. I don't know in whom or what I trusted, but I knew in my body that I was exactly where I was meant to be.

After an amount of time that I find impossible to say – half an hour? an hour? two hours? – I noticed that glowing shop windows were speeding past me, and I realised that I was on Regent Street. I felt myself slowing down and getting off my bike, wheeling it onto the pavement as I looked into the windows. I came to a set of windows which were frosted, opaque, mysterious. I stopped, sensing that I had reached my destination. I locked my bike in a rack nearby and walked back towards the windows.

As I approached, the windows opened, like a stage curtain, to let me through. I felt myself pulled inside, and as I crossed the threshold I realised that I was inside the showroom of the CybLife Corporation, man-ufacturers of – among other products – the CybFriends range.

3.

My memory is strange. When I try to recall the details of my visit to the showroom, I cannot picture the unadulterated memory of the visit itself. What comes to mind, however hard I try, is overlaid with the memory of a morning in bed with Grace, months later, just before the hearing. I was reading a document we had just received from CybLife as part of the case: *Exhibit 52 – Export from CybLife Data Cube*[*], which was the corporation's record of the key events occurring during my visit to the showroom.

'It's funny' I remember saying to Grace, as I scanned it. 'There are lots of inaccuracies in this document, but even if all the details were correct, this account would do no justice whatsoever to what actually happened.'

'What do you mean, *what actually happened*?'

'What happened to me!'

'Ah! So your take on it is what actually happened, is it?' she had teased me.

If I hadn't been so into her, I would probably have found that comment very irritating. But I liked her teasing; I found myself wrapping myself around her, holding her extra tightly, in mock restraint. We stayed like that for quite a while, as I read the document more carefully to myself.

Starting at the top, with the section beginning *Data source: showroom 001*, this is what I understood the document to be saying:

- *Sensors embedded in the walls of the entrance hallway detect a prospect – me – entering the showroom.*
- *My age is likely between thirty and thirty-five.*
- *The facial recognition software does not recognise an existing account.*
- *I walk tentatively.*
- *No wearables or other devices are identified.*
- *Some factor extrapolated from the above means I am assumed to have low purchase intent and results in my allocation to the Bronze band, which triggers the launch of the Bronze Prospect Conversion routine.*

As I read this, I felt angry. 'Grace, this is outrageous!' I found myself exclaiming.

'What is?'

63

'All of it! They tried to identify my face without asking for permission! And how dare they assume anything about my intentions!'

She rolled her eyes as if to say 'What do you expect?'

Given what I have since learned about the corporation, these aspects seem trivial. What still strikes me, however, is the extent to which these immediate impressions of me were inaccurate. In fact:

- I was older than the exhibit suggested: forty-two. (Perhaps I seemed younger because some of my wrinkles were hidden by the dark glasses I was wearing to cocoon myself from the outside world.)
- I already held an account with CybLife, which had required me to submit a photo (though I had signed up under an alias). I had created this account as part of my substantial research online into the product ranges: watching videos, reading reviews. I had even filled in a 'Which CybFriend is right for you?' questionnaire, using the alias. (Presumably the glasses prevented the cross-matching of the images.)
- While my gait was tentative, this reflected my general flat mood at the time, which was a key reason I was motivated to make the purchase. I actually had very strong intent to purchase, as per the sense of boldness I described above.

I carried on, silently reading the next section of the Exhibit – *Stage 1: Prospect Interception protocol* – which covered the next few moments of my visit to the showroom. This is what I took the document to be saying:

- *The first stage – Prospect Interception protocol - of the Bronze Prospect Conversion routine is launched.*
- *An available customer service agent – number 277 – is assigned to the task of assisting me with the potential purchase.*
- *Agent 277 allows me seven seconds of uninterrupted browsing time.*
- *During this time, I enter the personalised health department, walk past the new CogEnhancer™ range, and stop in front of the CybFriends™ display.*
- *Once the seven seconds have elapsed, agent 277 approaches me and asks something, maybe 'Are you looking for anything in particular?'*
- *I am deemed to have low interest in engaging in conversation.*

As I lay there, reading the document, wrapped around Grace, I was remembering what was actually going on for me at the time. I did not share any of this with her, but knowing her, she could probably sense the emotional tone of what I was remembering. I stroked her gloves, softly.

- As I got to the CybFriends section, I got distracted by a customer services assistant coming towards me. It was her figure which first struck me: my eyes must have lingered for longer than it took to read her badge:

YASMIN
HERE FOR YOU

- I realised she was talking to me – her voice detectably synthetic but nonetheless suggestive – so I looked up. Catching her intensely green almond-shaped eyes, I felt embarrassed, averted my gaze and lost the ability to behave naturally.
- I had not heard what she had asked me so I mumbled 'Umm... this is my first visit', hoping that fitted the question.

I squeezed Grace very tightly. Thinking how different she was from Yasmin, I marvelled, yet again, at how surprising my feelings for her were. They were surprising to me, at least.

Note

* **EXHIBIT 52 – EXPORT FROM CYBLIFE DATA CUBE**

Data source: showroom 001
Sensor location: customer entrance
Date: 07.10.2025
Time: 19:22:43
Scanning prospect profile…
Age: 30 - 35 years (80% confidence)
Facial ID data match: failed
Assign Prospect ID: X2715A2
Gait: stride profile 3 - TENTATIVE
Devices & Wearables: none detected
Derived purchase intent: LOW
Assign prospect category: BRONZE
Launch Bronze Prospect Conversion routine

Stage 1: Prospect Interception protocol
Event: Searching for available Bronze Level Customer Service agent…
Event: Requesting agent 277…
Event: Agent 277 accepted
Event: Agent 277 beginning 7 seconds non-approach time
Event: Agent 277 geo-tracking prospect
Detecting…
… Prospect entering Personalised Health
… Prospect passing CogEnhancer range
… Prospect walking pace dropping 67%
… Prospect stationary by CybFriends 5.0
Event: Agent 277 approRetrieving data. Wait for a few seconds, then try cutting or copying again.aching
Detecting…
… Prospect gaze towards CybFriends 5.0
Event: Agent 277 executing verbal approach
Detecting…
… Prospect mode: casual browsing

CARLA JENKINS

Fifty Minutes

Synopsis

Fifty Minutes *is a general fiction novel about Dani, a young woman who seeks justice after being exploited by her psychotherapist.*

London, 2019. Dani, a troubled twenty-year-old university dropout, decides to seek help for her eating disorder so she can return to university and finish her degree. She starts having psychotherapy with Richard Goode. When he encourages her to confront painful truths, she flirts with him as a distraction. Dani is attracted to this esteemed professional, thirty years her senior, and in awe of how well-educated and knowledgeable he is.

In her new stable environment, living with her sister, working in a restaurant kitchen and beginning to engage with her therapy, Dani feels her life is coming together. This changes when she has sex with Richard during a therapy session. They begin an affair which soon becomes a maelstrom of manipulation and fight for control.

When Dani discovers that Richard has had sexual relationships with many of his clients, using the secrets they revealed to him in therapy as blackmail, she is disgusted. Richard tells Dani that she is different, that he is in love with her, but she reports him to the professional standards authority. They attend a hearing where Richard denies all of the allegations, and convincingly describes Dani as a fantasist. Due to insufficient evidence, Richard walks away with his reputation intact and free to carry on practising. Dani's anger at the injustice consumes her, and she is determined to find a way to stop Richard from exploiting more of his female clients.

Dani attempts to make contact with Richard's previous clients but keeps hitting walls until she meets Anya. Dani persuades her to report him. This time there is enough evidence to prove Richard's guilt.

ONE
Monday 14th January 2019
The reason I chose Richard Goode was proximity. He's a twenty-minute walk away, a few minutes by bus, or one stop on the tube. He lives closest.

'You're early; would you like to sit in the waiting room? It's just around the corner.' He motions with his hand to the side of the building. I look at my phone. It's five to six.

'I'll come back.'

As I walk down the path, I feel self-conscious about my tight jeans, and I wish he'd close the door. It clicks shut as I reach the gate. I take a pouch of tobacco from my bag, sit on the low brick wall and roll a thin cigarette. I smoke under the light of the street lamp until six o'clock exactly. Then I knock again.When I booked the initial appointment, I didn't know about 'boundaries': start on time; don't run over; don't try to rearrange the appointment. Psychotherapists should provide *consistency*, *predictability* and *security* for their clients which means the same place, the same hour and a calm environment.

The second time he answers, he doesn't say anything, just turns and walks down the hallway to a room on the left. People bang on about the beauty of sunrises and sunsets, but I've never seen one that's affected me like the sight of a wall of books. Nobody I know has such a collection, and I've only seen this many before in a library or bookshop. Two of the walls are lined from floor to ceiling with shelves, a muted rainbow of thick and thin spines. Expensive looking brown leather armchairs face each other, and there's the therapist's couch with a green checked blanket folded at the end. Beautiful pictures hang on the walls. One is made of lots of squares with either dots or criss-crosses inside, in shades of beige and brown. Another's of deep blue arcs and light green dashes. There's only one picture of people: a watercolour, smaller than A4. It's a girl sitting on her father's lap. The girl's face is partly hidden by the father's arm, and the father is stroking the girl's hair. There's a faint smell of leather. I stand and absorb it all. I don't have to think about my breathing. Sometimes the only way to get a deep enough breath is to make myself yawn.

'You may hang your coat here.'

He gestures to the hat stand. I'm not sure where to sit, and I don't want to get it wrong. I keep my coat on and sit on the chair which has a box of tissues on the table next to it. I put my bag by my feet. He sits on the chair opposite and crossing his legs, leans back and clasps his hands together, resting them on his brown corduroy thigh. I'm pleased with what he's wearing; it seems like the type of thing a psychotherapist should wear; corduroy trousers, in earthy tones. His trouser leg has ridden up. He's wearing yellow and grey diamond socks, and I wonder if he's got lots of pairs in different colours. I look up to see he's observing me and I'm embarrassed that he caught me staring at his ankle.

It's so still in this room, and the air is nice and cool. I should say something.

'Alright?'

His chin moves down and up again slightly, not quite a nod, more an acknowledgement that I've spoken, filled the space a little with that one word.

Looking at the bookshelves, I tilt my head so I can read the titles on the spines: *Clinical Notes on Disorders of Childhood; Psychotherapy: An Erotic Relationship – Transference and Counter Transference Passions; Class and Psychoanalysis: Landscapes of Inequality.* My neck begins to ache, so I stop.

'Oh.' I take four twenties from my bag and walk over to him. 'Eighty pounds for today, yeah?' I hold the money towards him, but he doesn't take it. 'I thought I'd pay you now in case you're worried I won't, after the session I mean.'

He doesn't say anything. He doesn't take the money. I feel stupid, holding my arm out. I briefly consider letting the notes flutter to the floor, but I put them on the table next to his chair and sit down.

'Why would I think that?'

'What?'

'That you wouldn't pay?'

'Because I could. I could get away without paying – if I decide not to come back.'

I sit up straighter. I've never been in a room like this. I feel a better person for being in it. I read more of the book titles.

'You've got a lot of books.'

He doesn't answer.

'You like reading.'

I carry on reading the book titles, which all seem to be about psychotherapy or philosophy. A light green spine with *French Grammar in Context* stands out.

'Do you speak French?'

Nothing.

I change the inflection.

'Do you speak French?'

He frowns.

'Vouz parlez-français?'

He stifles a laugh.

We sit in silence until it's broken by a low rumbling. I wonder what he had for lunch. Probably something like a quinoa salad or sea-bass with lightly steamed vegetables. Whatever it was, it wasn't enough, and he's still hungry, or he ate too close to six, and he's mid-digestion. There's no other sound in the room except a clock ticking. This time there's a low gurgling noise. I wait for him to say something, but he shows no sign of having noticed. I can feel myself blushing. He should eat before, or not eat before, or do whatever he needs to not to be making these noises in my space, my time. This is costing me eighty quid an hour, not even a real hour, a therapist's hour, which is fifty minutes. I'm paying practically two quid a minute. I've just spent two quid on listening to his stomach.

I study the painting of the girl sitting on her father's lap. I think about how the girl, leaning so far into her father's chest, would be breathing in the smell of his jumper. I wonder if she'd experience his jumper as soft or scratchy against her cheek, if she could feel his heart beating. I raise my eyebrows and smile at my therapist, but he doesn't smile. Fuck him.

'My Dad would've got up and left the room at your stomach making noises like that.'

His nose moves like he's caught a strange smell in the air.

'We weren't allowed to make any noise when we were eating. Dad would go mental. Once, during dinner, my mum burped with her mouth closed. She had to leave the room before the fall-out.'

I take my bag from my feet and put in on my lap. I find my phone and check the time. It's quarter past six. Richard Goode has hardly said anything, and I want my money's worth from this session.

'What do you think of that? Him hating noises like that?'

'Misophonia,' he says eventually.

'What?'

'Misophonia. A strong aversion to particular sounds.'

'Okay, I didn't come here to speak about my Dad, though. He died last year.' I shake my head. 'It's alright.'

I picture sitting at the table with Dad, smoking and playing cards or Scrabble. Then I remember how often he used to call me a *fucking piece of shit*. When I make a mistake, they're the words that come; *You fucking piece of shit*. I might ask Richard how I can stop this.

'Where did you go just then?'

His voice is gentle. Richard Goode is strong, with his broad chest and wide shoulders. He's wearing a thin jumper over a shirt, close-fitting enough to see that there's not a hint of fat. I reckon he's in his late forties, but he's fit. An attractive man in an attractive room. I scratch the back of my neck.

'I don't want to talk about my Dad. I want to talk about the bulimia. I need to get it under control. I had to drop out of uni because of it.'

He does the half nod again.

'I tried Cognitive Behaviour Therapy. I had ten sessions in a group with two other girls. I was referred by my GP, and the counsellor, the woman running it, was lovely, and it worked, for a while but then I swapped one bad behaviour for another. I think, from reading about it, that psychotherapy's more effective at getting to the root of a problem and changing it that way, and that's what I need.'

He raises his chin.

'I need to tell you firstly Dani, that this is a safe space and everything you tell me will be treated as confidential unless I feel you are at harm to yourself and then I would have a duty to report it.'

'Fair enough.' I nod. I want to get started.

'Psychotherapy is about exploring your feelings and understanding them. If you have the courage to be honest, curious and vulnerable during the sessions, you will maximise your progress, but it will take time. And sometimes it can be painful, and difficult feelings will arise, but I am here to guide and support you.'

He speaks so slowly. I try and slow myself down so I can pace my speech like his, but my words come out in a rush, as usual.

'It's what I need.'

'I offer person-centred psychotherapy, which means it is important we focus on the 'here and now,' and exploring what is happening between us. What you have already bought to the session reveals to me that one of the areas we need to address is your relationship with others –'

'I already said I don't want to talk about my Dad. Sorry, sorry, I interrupted you. Go on.'

'What you have already bought to the session indicates to me that one of the areas it would be helpful to address is your relationships with others, however, and this is entirely natural, as your accounts of them may be biased, it is most useful to concentrate on the one relationship of which I do have the most precise knowledge, and that is our relationship, and what occurs between you and I in this room.'

'Yeah, okay.' I feel the toes of my left foot curling when he says, 'the relationship between you and I.' I look at his chest and try and match my breathing to the rise and fall. 'I need to sort out the bulimia though.'

I can tell he's thinking about what I've said. You can tell when someone's listened.

'You need to 'sort out' your bulimia. Dani, I wonder if you make yourself sick because you do not know how to deal with your emotions in a healthy way?'

'That's it! That is it exactly, it's what I need to work on, why I'm here. I need to sort it out so I can get back to university and finish my degree.'

Keeping eye contact after I've finished speaking feels too intimate. I focus on his hands which rest on the arms of his chair. They're large, clean. There's no wedding ring.

'Education, being educated, is important to you.'

'I'll be the first one in my family to do it. I need to learn. I'd love a room like this one day, so many books...' I want to go and run my fingers along the spines. 'There's no books where I'm living now, well, I keep some in my bedroom, but it's not really my bedroom. I'm staying with my sister Jo and her fiancé Stevie, and his daughter comes to stay every other weekend. She's only three, and Stevie's old-fashioned so you can imagine what the bedroom is like...lots of pastel colours, dolls, teddy bears.' I start to talk faster when I see there's only five minutes of the session left. 'I don't want you to think I'm ungrateful or for it to seem like I'm complaining. Jo's doing me a huge favour letting me live with them, and she's not even charging me rent, she's helping me get back on track. It's why I can afford to come here.'

Fifty minutes of Richard Goode's professional services costs as much as I earn in a day. Eight hours of pot wash for fifty minutes with him, but it's fair. My work is unskilled, minimum wage, anyone could do it. Psychotherapists are highly educated, have years of training and are very knowledgeable.

'Dani, what are you doing?'

I put my bag back on the floor.

'I was checking what time it was.'

'But why didn't you take your phone out to check? I assume you were looking at your phone?'

'I didn't want you to think I was being rude. I haven't got a watch, and I can't see a clock in here, although I can hear one...is that one?'

I point to the mantlepiece. It looks like a little travel clock, but it's angled to face him. I lean forward and think about what to say. His eyes go to the clock, and he uncrosses his legs.

'And we'll have to leave it there for today.'

I stand and try to smile.

'Right. Thanks.'

Our eyes don't meet because he's looking towards the window, even though the blind is down. He stands up, walks across the room and opens the door for me. Waits there, with his fingers on the handle. When I get to the door, I pause. I only come up to his shoulder. I want to rest my forehead against his chest.

MARGARET JENNINGS

The Worry List

Synopsis

*The **unnamed central character** who is an unreliable witness, tried to exact revenge on her abusive father when she was only a child. A self-harming anorexic, she talks of her relationship with the child she lost in early pregnancy.*

*The **Woman Who Does Not Exist** serves as foil with whom our central character discusses her worries about religion and God. The protagonist reveals that she put blood in her father's ear when she was a child in order to make him think that he had had a brain haemorrhage. This scene, and the subsequent assault on her mother, replay in the narrator's story.*

***Mr. Via,** a local shopkeeper, tries to help the unnamed central character. **Her Husband** also tried to help her but has disappeared from her life.*

She believes that Mr. Via has two wives, one in India and one who plays rugby. A newspaper article frightens her, and she runs to Mr. Via's shop in desperation. She ends up hospitalised but refuses to talk to the psychiatrist.

The unnamed central character and Mr. Via set about finding the space in the house where she believes evil lurks. She begins to doubt the motives of both Mr. Via and The Woman Who Does Not Exist. The house is behaving strangely though it is unclear whether this is a haunting or caused by her anxiety. Hospitalised once more, she gets the help she needs. However, when the secret room is found, she is thrown back into the reality of her past as if it were really happening. She tries to murder her father because she believes she is in the past where he caused so much harm to her mother. Sadly, the person she kills is Mr. Via.

Chapter One

Love Haiku

Our love was hormones.
Nought but the play of nature
demanding rebirth.

The Worry List

Things forgotten
Things remembered
Things people said
Things I said.

The way the wind flaps
on a still day.

A crow and a squirrel on a lawn.
An empty bird box.
A drop – virtual, literal, surreal,
a prescient fall

That one thing.
I am going to die.

The way she fell and left me. The accidental flush. The realisation of loss
too late to say farewell. He says not to cry. That nature knows what to
waste. 'Let me not to the marriage of true minds admit impediments. Love
is not love which alteration finds.' Alteration. Finds.

She, who lives in me. Tainted by his words that speak of error; mis-
make, mistake. Replay. She was... she was... she was. Was! Is!

Hold time now. Close to my skin. Close to the leak of milk meant for
you.

There is a tune in my head.
It will take no notation
on five lines with a clef.
It is. It is. It is.
A white line.
That runs and runs

and runs.
An un-parallel
parallelogram.
No crash.

A FRONT COMING THROUGH

The garden chairs know only empty. Summer long they grow green moulds in happy anticipation of visitors who never come. Blue skies yield vainglorious hope. Starlight is music and lust free. Snail slime tracks white across the green moulds, write some uninterpretable language of loneliness in a garden that should be bee buzzing, flower zapping, scent intoxicating, fun.

In winter things ice over. There is a thin crust over water. The garden chairs are not put away under cover. They must cope as best they can. At least the snails have gone into hiding.

It is not a question of years or seasons however. It is an era of perpetuity. It is grandiose in its longevity and demeaned by its own existence.
The garden chairs know only empty, the warm wind knows only cold, the summer sun is blinded by its own light, there is no end, no resolution to eternity. No full stop

A front is coming through.

EMPTY

He empties me daily as if I were a piggy bank. He ignores the ducats and the gold sovereigns, he is after the shonky coins, the fifty pence pieces that will not weight a parking metre, the pounds that are only detected on the humiliation of a set of bank scales. He finds them of course. All of them. All the frauds and duplicities and even the simple mistakes and he points them out. Slowly and carefully so that I might understand more easily. And swear to do better.

I sit on the swing today and look at the sky. I am an adult woman and I only just fit between the hurt of the chains. The playground is empty because it is a cold day, and too early in the morning for children to be up and about.

I imagine them snuggled under blankets. Parents lingering at the door to admire the beauty of their children's being as they sleep. The same parents padding quietly to the kitchen to enjoy quiet awake time before the chaos commences. Today is a school day. To get to the school, some will choose to walk through the park.

I cannot be here then. That would look peculiar. But now I luxuriate in the beauty of the medley of greys in a winter sky and watch my ghost

75

child playing – she is holding the chains of the swing beside me. She cannot get on the swing on her own and once she is on, I will have to push her. I say she can sit on mummy's lap. She comes over and I feel the weight of her as I lift her, I feel the weight of her on my lap, yet she is not there.

He would accuse me, if he knew of these moments, of keeping false coins so close to my side that they are invisible to him. I think that if ever he truly walked with me, if ever he weighed every one of my words for sadness, instead of weighing them for error, he would see the child too.

I am glad he does not do that, for he might want her gone. Might say that she is an error of my psyche that needs to be exorcised. Gone. That is worry number one. That he might have the power to make my daughter disappear and never come back to me. That he might use the power I give him, the power he uses to sort the coinage of my usefulness, to disenfranchise my daughter. To cannibalise me somehow, so she does not exist any more. I know she is not real. I know she is not flesh and blood. But that does not stop me feeling the weight of her as she sits on my lap on the swing. Her hair is tickling my face as it is caught by a chill morning breeze. It does not stop me reaching down for her hand as we cross the road and practice the drill, look left, look right, look left again. She is mine in my reality and I will hold onto her forever. I will not have her used as a weight and measure of my sanity. I will repeat, I know she is not real. But I also know that she walks with me.

I have some bubbles in my coat pocket. I take them out and release the wand and blow the magic into the sky. I marvel at the way the colours twist and shimmer and entice. I watch them as they pop one by one. A bubble lands on the swing and refuses to pop. It remains there shimmering like gossamer and I watch my child clapping her hands and laughing and living in a moment that never was. Never was, for her or for me.

A woman, stiffened by a winter coat, walks past. She stutters a bit in the pace of her walk when she sees me. It is an eloquent silence and I make to move. Should I just wave in a friendly fashion as if I am waiting for someone? Should I leave as if I was just resting for a moment. She has noticed the bubbles. She is too far away for me to see what she is thinking. She is too close for me to be unafraid that she will report my strange behaviour to someone with the power to stop me. Perhaps word will get back to my husband and he will weigh those coins again and take even more of the duplicates and falsehoods from me. Sometimes self deceit keeps us warm.

I decide on a charm offensive. I walk up to this woman and ask what breed her dog is, what is his or her name. Tell her that I once owned a dog and sometimes I come to the park just to relive the days when we walked here. Yes, a long time ago, yes, she would not remember. Sorry about the swing and the bubbles but my hip was hurting, old running injury and I needed to sit down and I just happened to find the bubbles still in my pocket from a children's party at the weekend. I have always loved watching bubbles has she?

And she tells me of her children and her grandchildren and parties and bubbles and slides and holidays and the tiredness of being when children hold onto every hour of your every day. We talk for so long her dog lays down and tries to sleep, then gets up and whines. This is, of course, a chill winter morning, he or she wants to be off chasing a ball and going home to warmth and breakfast.

Eventually the woman walks away and thanks me for the nice chat, says she hopes to see me again. I nod and agree and say must get on, lots to do. And I leave. But there is not lots to do. I do not have to get on. I do not want to see that woman again. Every last word I said to her was a lie. I hope she walks away convinced that every word was true. I must be more careful if I sit on this swing again. I must just do it for the shortest time. I must watch my daughter run and play and laugh for the shortest time.

I am angry with this woman with a dog for shortening my time with my imaginary daughter. I am angry with my husband for counting coins and always finding me wanting. I am angry with the cold wind for whispering with the trees in such a conspiratorial way.

Worry Number one. I must not be found out.

I never say my name out loud. I don't want just anyone to know it. You will never know my name.

My home is a ridiculous place. It is mock something or other. Mock gothic? It is hard stone imported at great cost from another part of the country. It is spires and pinnacles and arches with pointy tops and it is a treachery too. Inside there is softness and warmth and colours chosen by someone else, from a tasteful palette. I am a latecomer to the story of its being and this house treats me in an off hand way as if I am soon to be gone.

How can she know? But the house tells me to go by cluttering corners with nets of spiders webs, and throwing leaves through the back door in autumn and making beams creak when no-one is walking on them and letting the wind say words as she passes through.

I am a latecomer to my husband's life too. This house was mine before he was. Decorated by a more adept hand. I have standards to live up to.

This is a place of demands and judgement. She, this house, sits in gardens and wears the lawn as a large skirt. Flower borders are the frills at the bottom. Each dead flower is a piece of caught lace. Her eyes, where are her eyes? They are not the windows for they gleam with the bought cleanliness created by the window cleaner. Her eyes should be mean and keen to find fault. Perhaps they hide above the black guttering. That's to the outside – the insides are closed curtains. Pretending to be shut yet watching everything.

This cold morning, with the dog owner reassured of my sanity, I walk home via the shops. Mr Via always welcomes me as a friend, asks how my day is, and the weather. Today he says that I am up early, couldn't sleep? No, I reply, thoughts woke me up and he starts telling me about the things in his life that keep him awake and he cannot stay awake for he has a business to run, and if he doesn't do it who will, so he has a special tape by his bed, would I like the name I can get the name for you. I say yes that would be lovely and hope that he forgets this conversation by the evening and is simply happy to allow me to pay for the paper and the milk and the sweets now.

'Your child must have a sweet tooth' he says as he hands them back to me. He rests his hands on the counter and watches me leave the shop. I know he does, even though I cannot see him. I know he does because he is wondering about this child who he never sees yet is always having sweets bought as a surprise. I know he shakes his head at the worry of my being someone to worry about, tells himself off for being so silly and walks back to the shelf he was restocking. Walks back to keeping an ear open for the clang of the bell that says someone has entered the shop. I wonder if that sound visits him in his sleep. I wonder if it is a nightmare; whether it introduces each cast member of his nocturnal dream meanderings.

No matter, I go back to the house. My house.

PETER LEWENSTEIN

Burned

Synopsis

Burned *is a story about two suspicious deaths that happened fifty years apart. The victims are related and by the end, we learn the killers are connected too. It is set in Ghana.*

A retired engineer has been electrocuted. **Patrice Le Congo**, *an intrepid human rights defender, is asked to investigate. He learns that the victim was being threatened by people who want to build a huge solar farm on his land. The only witness to what happened was the victim's cousin,* **Auntie Yawor**, *an elderly woman who suffers from dementia and is traumatised by events of the past.*

In 1966, a time of coup plots and Cold War politics, Yawor was involved in an investigation of her own, into the death of her sister, who was knocked down by a hit-and-run driver. Yawor discovered the culprit was an American spy who was helping a group of police and army officers with a plan to overthrow the government. For this reason, the police protected him, and he got away with his crime.

Patrice finds out the people behind the solar farm are involved in a plot to blow up the Akosombo Dam. He prevents the attack, which was being led by an American who is killed but who, it turns out, had at one time worked for the CIA. An accomplice got away. He's an older man, who now runs a luxury hotel on the coast.

In the climax to the novel, Patrice goes to the hotel with Auntie Yawor, who recognises the old man as the man who killed her sister fifty years earlier. The man confirms it was his colleague who killed the engineer. They had been contracted by the CIA, which was subversively supporting attempts to expand American solar-power production in Africa.

Ghana
1966

She's running. Doesn't know where. Anywhere. Get away.

A screech of tyres. She glances back. Headlights swing on to the wide, deserted road. He's coming after her.

She scrambles down into the deep ditch by the roadside. Squats at the bottom, over a trickle of black water. Panting.

79

The car approaches, roars past. She listens as it disappears into the distance. He'll be back. He won't stop till he finds her, not now she knows.

She can't stay where she is but she can't catch her breath. She hangs her head. Stares at her dress, that's clinging to her thighs. Before she has time to move, she hears the car again.

It gets closer, slows to a crawl, stops. A door opens.

She lies next to the black trickle, pressed against the side of the ditch, under a slight overhang. Footsteps approach, scrunches of shoes on gravel. They come to a stop, almost on top of her. They don't move. She can hear him breathing. She closes her eyes, but pictures him standing there, stroking his moustache.

He coughs, goes back to the car. Slams the door. Makes her jump. Then he drives off.

This time she has to go. Starts to climb up the side of the ditch. Loses her footing. Slips. Her bag falls off her shoulder and spills open at the bottom. Panting again, she gathers up the contents, stuffs everything back in the bag. Clambers back up, and out.

Looks and listens. No cars. Crosses the road; more trees that side, more shadows. Runs from one to the next, till she reaches the avenue. Looks one way. Can't go there, he'll search for her there for sure. She's got no choice. Looks the other way, the way home. She sets off, keeping to the grassy verge.

Music. An electric guitar, drums. The band at the hotel. She thinks for a moment she can hide there, amongst the crowd. But her dress, the mud. She'll go home. Tell them everything. Do something good, for a change. She reaches her turning, but she can't do it. Can't face them.

She walks on. Doesn't know where. Anywhere.

One or two cars drive past. Another comes, doesn't drive past. Slows right down. She knows it's him. Glances to the side. He's behind her. She reaches another turning. Steps out to cross. He comes round the corner.

She runs, down the road.

Same screech of tyres.

She looks back as she runs. She's staring into the headlights.

Fifty years later

He offers his arm for support and she takes it, and smiles. A rare moment of recognition. The old songs seem to have roused her.

They walk up by the river, in the bright sunlight, till they reach the dam. A stream of water is gushing out of the sluice. He offers to help her sit down on a rock but she waves him aside with a mutter and a frown and he leaves her standing with her crutch.

He goes inside the powerhouse. He picks up the cable ends and holds them up in his hands and shouts out through the open door. 'When in a few moments I turn the switch … Remember, Cousin?' She's old now, often lost in her own world, but if she can hear him, then she might. 'Our very own Akosombo! We will dedicate it to Osagyefo and to Adzo.'

'And Ofori!' she says, shouting back above the sound of the water.

So, she does remember something of that time. He inspects the connections. Gently, he blows off some specks of dust. He hears a rustle behind him, but at the same time he's distracted by a sharp movement outside. He looks up. She's waving her crutch in the air.

'Ofori, come!' she cries. 'Ofori!'

She must be confused. It was all so long ago. He nods back to her solemnly, hoping to calm her, and says, 'To those we lost.'

Chapter 1

The taxi sped down the brightly-lit six-lane highway, past neon-crested shopping malls and high-rise apartment buildings. Patrice watched the Accra nightscape flash by. He checked his phone. His boss had told him to come around eight. She said she just wanted to ask him something – which sounded ominous. She was a formidable woman and accustomed to getting her own way.

They swept through a set of open gates and on to a cobbled drive and came to a halt outside the hotel. He climbed the carpeted marble stairs. Two shining sheets of plate glass swung open and he walked past two doormen in tunics, standing to attention. He spotted Josie Mwinga chatting to one of the receptionists. She was wearing a well-cut western dress and had had her hair done, straightened. She seemed to like being in this city. Staying in a place like this probably made her like it even more.

'Ah, Patrice,' she said, turning. 'Good, thank you for coming. Come and have something to eat. The food here is very good.' She led him through to a restaurant, a large room of pillars and chandeliers. 'I recommend the buffet. I know you like Ghanaian food and they will cook your fish fresh, in front of you.'

The chef fried up fillets of tilapia and carp and Patrice added portions of jollof rice, grated gari, fried plantain and boiled yam. He carried his plate over to Mwinga's table and sat down opposite. She'd chosen meat. As he ate, he felt her eyes watching him.

'Tell me Patrice, what did you think of the conference? I know you didn't want to come. I expect you're itching to get back to the field?'

'Well, I don't know about that, Ma'am ...'

'Patrice, please call me Josie, you know me well enough.'

'Yes, Josie …' Even making a polite request, she barked out the words like an order. 'It's true I don't enjoy meetings. I find it hard to stay awake, especially after lunch. But it's been good to have a break. And I've always wanted to come to Ghana. As a matter of fact …'

'You know the discrimination suffered by disabled people is a very serious issue. That's why the African Union's Human Rights Commission organised this event, and why we thought it important that you and some of the other investigators came.'

'Yes, of course.' Patrice was becoming more suspicious by the mouthful. They'd had a team briefing earlier, at the end of the conference. She can't have got him over here just to repeat what she'd said then. But the food was delicious.

'Anyway, Patrice, I'm glad you like it here. There's something I need you to do for me.' She chewed some food and took a sip of beer.

He was getting a sinking feeling. 'Actually, I have some plans, I want to …'

'It has to do with the conference, in a way. You remember that friend of mine I told you about, George Abotsi, whose cousin suffered all sorts of abuse, because she walked with a limp? Her name was Yawor, I think.'

'I'm not sure I do.' Patrice put down his fork.

'Probably you weren't listening to me. Well, it's very sad. I rang this afternoon to arrange to go to see him, and his daughter told me he'd died, a week ago. He was electrocuted.'

'Electrocuted?'

'I feel so bad I didn't contact him before the conference …'

'What happened?'

'I don't know the details. The line was very bad. It didn't really make sense and I was so taken aback … But one thing I heard very clearly; she said it wasn't an accident.'

Patrice was getting a strong sense of déjà vu. He looked at Josie Mwinga as she ate her food, apparently unconcerned she was asking him to do something in his own time.

'So, will you go there to meet her?' she asked, wiping her mouth. 'It's not far from Accra … What's the matter? Why are you looking like the sky has fallen down?'

'I was planning a trip myself, to western Ghana.'

'You can still do that. Just go to see this woman and help her calm down. You have to go because I told her you'd be there in the morning. I would go myself but I have meetings with government officials here in Accra and it's very important we follow up on the conference outcomes while people are still thinking about it. You can go there and be back here by the afternoon and then set off on your trip.'

He pouted his lips, doubtfully. 'I don't see how I'll be able to help. If there is foul play, then she must call the police.'

'She didn't say there was foul play. She just said it wasn't an accident. Please don't be difficult about this, Patrice. She needs someone to talk to. Sit with her, let her say what it is she needs to say and then when things are clear to you what's actually happened, then you can advise her on the right course of action.'

He thought it through. Delaying his trip wasn't the issue, but with Josie Mwinga, one thing often led to another. 'Will I be paid for this? You know I'm on leave now ...'

'Paid?' Her voice was getting louder. 'Well, really, are you adding up your hours? I'm asking you for a favour, and you're asking for money? Do you want double-time, perhaps?'

'A favour? You've used that word before.'

'Yes, a favour. We're a team, we support each other. I want the people in my team to be committed ...'

'You think I'm not committed? I nearly got killed in Cameroon, helping you, remember? When those farmers were massacred?'

'I didn't say you're not committed. I'm just saying ... well, I'm disappointed. I thought you were someone who was motivated by principles, not money.'

He looked at her, dumfounded. *'Mungu wangu!* My God! It's hard to believe you can think that either. But it doesn't matter. It's good. It means you won't miss me when I'm gone.'

Mwinga stopped chewing the piece of meat in her mouth. 'And what does that mean?'

'I've been meaning to tell you. I want to take some time off, a year perhaps, some study leave.'

'What?' she squawked, a look of disbelief on her face.

'Yes, well, I ... You see, in the course of my work, over the past few years, I've come across some very bad things. Terrible violence. People doing things to other people that you cannot imagine how they can do it. I need to understand ... what's going on, the bigger picture.'

She took a breath. 'Well, this is a surprise! There I was thinking you were anxious to get back to the field when what you want really is to go back to school. You ... you've barely been with us any time and now you're asking for a year off. I mean, I know your job is not easy, but come on, Patrice!'

'Well, that's fine, Ma'am … Josie, if it's a problem, I can quit.'

The large room seemed to fall silent for a moment, like when a waiter drops a pile of plates. He hadn't been meaning to raise the issue of study leave until he had it all organised. And he hadn't been meaning to threaten her with his resignation either, but now he'd done it, he felt strengthened. He knew how much the work of the Commission's Investigations Unit meant to his boss but he had to regain some control over his own life.

'Listen Patrice …' She was talking more quietly now. 'There's no need to make a hasty decision. I'm not saying it's a bad idea, for the future. But I'd need to discuss it … I don't know if I could keep your post open. I will try. But in return, will you help me, tomorrow? Please?'

'Okay,' he said, pleased he'd made his point. 'I'll go and talk to her.'

'Thank you, Patrice.' She clicked her fingers and ordered some more beer for them both. 'You know,' she said, brightly, as if everything was settled between them, 'the Abotsis are a well-known family. George was a government minister once upon a time and his father was a well-respected public servant.'

He started picking at his food again.

'Anyway,' she said, 'what is it that you have to go to western Ghana for?'

'I want to go to Nkroful. It's the birthplace of Kwame Nkrumah. He was one of my heroes when I was a student. It's actually been an ambition of mine to go there.'

'Oh, for heaven's sake, Patrice! You have the strangest notions. Not even Ghanaians are interested in that man. They got rid of him, you know, a long time ago. But it doesn't matter. You can still go, after you've seen this poor woman.'

ALAN MACGLAS

Beyond Bounds

Synopsis

*Bel is a young pianist living in London, working days as a dance company
repetiteur and evenings in a jazz club. The story opens with her exhibition
to a famous Russian maestro at Wigmore Hall and a visit to the nearby
Wallace Collection, giving an impression of assurance, talent and
education, which is enhanced by attendance at an exclusive supper party
where she discusses the nature and fragility of success with the Russian
maestro and his young wife. But contact with a former boyfriend brings
news that police are investigating allegations of misdeeds at the children's
home where they both grew up, exposing undercurrents of unease and
sexual tension.*

*Her life is upended when she is questioned by the police about
photographs apparently compromising her with her 'godfather', the
former head of her children's home, who disappeared seven years ago.*

*In the traumatic fall-out, Bel forms a bond with one of the company
dancers, Cat, who offers practical advice when Bel is invited to play at a
soirée in a country house. The host of this event tells her that he knew her
godfather, adding to the sense that her life is in the grip of unseen forces.*

*Back home, her friendship with Cat becomes intimate, and they sleep
together. Then Bel meets her former boyfriend's present partner, who
reveals more details about her godfather. She is also introduced to an
MI6 officer, who questions her about refugees who transited through the
children's home with her godfather's help.*

*At the climax of the story, Bel returns home to find her godfather
himself waiting for her. Over the next twenty-four hours they discuss their
shared history, before armed police arrive in the night to take him away,
leaving Bel to pick up the pieces of her life.*

Beyond Bounds

The drums and bass were securely stored, the vents exhaling the fumes of
sweat and drink, the janitor stripping the tablecloths out of the booths, the
owner in a mood because the bar takings were twenty pounds light, the
band-leader smoking a cigarette in the doorway as he waited for his wife,
she taking her time because she always did, though she had nothing to
pack, her only instrument being the voice still crooning in her throat, still

a little in love with the evening now over and the audience now gone, languidly calling, ''Night, Bel,' as she drifted out, adding, 'Good luck for tomorrow,' over her shoulder.

'Thanks. 'Night, Han.' Bel finished packing her music books, closed the piano keyboard cover, looked over the rest of the dais to make sure nothing had been left behind, shouldered her bag and followed.

Cars, buses and trains took people home through the lit suburban darkness, east to Woolwich and Charlton, west to Deptford and Rotherhithe, south to Lewisham, north through the Blackwall Tunnel.

Bel alone walked. Deep in her old jacket, companioned by her bag, she strode up past the park walls onto Blackheath, and there wandered in the expanse of civic grass, cleaning her nose of the club's stale air, her eyes of its spotlights, her ears of the music, breathing the mild cold wind. Walking alone on the heath at night was not something that normal young women felt safe to do, but Bel had never been normal.

When her head was clear, she went home to her dead teacher's flat in the Victorian terrace under the heath's flank, drank tea, reminded herself that the next day was special and important, didn't believe it, brushed her teeth, went to bed and slept the sleep of the young.

* * *

She was woken by the telephone, sounding from its table in the little hallway. Her heart lurched. The house phone ringing on dark mornings never brought good news. But surely by now she should be immune to tragedy. She rose, padded naked through to the hallway, switched on the table-lamp – a wooden boy holding up a box-shaped orange-screened lantern on a pole – picked up the phone and waited.

'That you, Bel?' From a background of voices, laughter, music.

'Yeah. Who zat?'

'What you mean, Who zat? Your favourite Aunty who it is.'

'Carrie!' She woke up properly. 'How are you? How's Jamaica?'

'Wonderful. I got company so I can't talk long.' Some indistinct conversation with a further voice – a tinny shriek of laughter. *'Sorry, Bel, what you say?'*

'I said, who's the company?'

'His name's Gilbert. He's a rascal.'

'Hey, are you getting laid?'

'This is the land of love, Bel.' More muffled laughter, and then Carina to someone aside: *'That is NOT TRUE – Bel, you hear what him saying about me?'*

'No, but I bet it's true.'

'It is NOT true... Anyway, how are you?'

'I'm fine. Some party you're having.' Bel glanced at the grandmother clock on the opposite wall as its dignified chime struck the hour. 'What time is it there?'

'Uh – two o'clock.'

'It's six here. I've got my exhibition this morning.' The information was lost in more noise. Bel waited for it to clear, then repeated: 'My exhibition's this morning.'

'Yeah, that's why I'm calling. To wish you luck. You show those people, sweetheart.'

'Thanks. How's Mo?'

'He's fine. He's asleep with Rosie. Curled up like two prawns in a wrap. They look so sweet. Shame they have to wake up and be horrible children. Listen, Bel: we're coming back Friday night. You wan' come round Saturday, help me shopping?'

Bel checked her work diary. 'Sure. I can meet you at the airport if you want.'

'Nah, we okay. I text you when we land. Love you Bel.'

'Love you Carrie. See you Saturday.'

Their voices parted between hot crowded laughing night-time Jamaica and cold lonely silent dawning London. Bel put the phone back on its rest, checked her diary again, then went to shower.

Granted normal service by the trains, she had plenty of time. With luck, she could get in some practice at the dance studios. Charles Peddie had told her to be at the Wigmore Hall by eleven, with a warning that she might have to wait an hour or more before Maestro Rakhin would hear her, and not to be surprised if she had to come away without playing at all.

She walked her usual route from Charing Cross to Soho, smelling the morning smells – damp wood, wet concrete and chemicals from a gutted building surrounded by scaffolding, hot pastries and coffee from cafés and sandwich shops, lemon and ammonia disinfectants, traffic fumes, spills of late-night takeaway food flavouring the swirl of gritty wind.

Her fingers were allowed one dose of coffee per morning. She got it from her usual source, the Casa Verdi, near Hollen Street. The proprietor glanced up and said automatically, 'Allo darlin, ow are you?' in an accent bred by Naples out of New Cross. He called all young women darling, and all young men young man. His flirting was innocuous: his wife worked alongside him, a diminutive olive-toned factor bustling with knives.

Bel exited with her carton of cappuccino, went round the corner, and entered the Hat Factory dance studios. She showed her pass to the security guard with a perfunctory, 'Hi,' to which he responded with a wary unsmiling, 'Morning.' He was new in the job. Men who didn't know her were generally disinclined to take chances, especially when they had to look up at her, which was usually the case.

She denied herself the lift and climbed the stairs two at a time to the practice studio. Janet the secretary was already in the office, greeting her with a wave of her talons, a bespectacled harrier dissecting a fresh kill of papers. Beside her was the company's guiding light, Dame Madeleine herself, a rare presence this early, muttering over some asinine correspondence, one hand knuckled on the silver-knobbed ebony cane that she used in public for elegance and only in private for support.

Janet frowned at the work rota. 'I thought you had an exhibition this morning? I've got Dorothy coming in to cover the classes.'

'It's not till eleven o'clock,' said Bel. 'I thought I'd borrow the piano for an hour. If that's okay.'

'I've a couple of squabs in there waiting to astonish me,' said Dame Madeleine absently. 'Play them something to loosen their knickers.' She glanced up at Bel. 'And good luck with Maestro Rakhin, darling. He's a moody bugger, I've heard.'

Bel didn't care, as long as he listened. Her teacher had always warned her she had to be twice as good as anybody else because the world was not fair.

She found three dancers already exercising in the studio. Two of them were Dame Madeleine's squabs, scared children – which was to say, a year or two younger than Bel – awaiting their trial. She greeted them with a friendly grin, for which they seemed grateful, smiling back with white teeth and wide panicked eyes.

She did not greet the third dancer, already absorbed in the reverie of warm-up: a torch-haired Glaswegian tough, the company's star *prima ballerina assoluta*, the apple of Dame Madeleine's eye and, at this hour of the morning, a notorious bitch. Interrupting her routine got much the same reaction as disturbing a leopard at her kill.

Bel knew about tough girls. She'd grown up with plenty.

She settled at the piano and played Bach, music to discipline the fingers and mind. The dancers didn't care what she played, as long as it had a definite rhythm.

More of the company drifted in, stripped and began to warm up, chattering and laughing. Dorothy arrived, was surprised to see Bel there, checked that she was indeed on duty, and disappeared to gossip in the office. Bel played on, neither looking at her hands nor taking notice of the dancers but engrossed in some mental space of her own.

Eventually she stopped, checked her watch and swung herself round on the stool to pick up her bag.

'Hey.'

Surprised, she looked up, straight into the green stare of leopard eyes.

'Oh, hi, Cat.'

Lines of perspiration were wandering down the sides of the dancer's face, but otherwise she was as cold as a Madonna. Cat wore no make-up in the mornings. Something they had in common.

'Can I ask a favour.' The hoarse Glasgow-bred voice did not invite refusal.

'Sure.'

'That Bach you're playing. I'm planning some solo work on that kind of music. Counterpoint. Can you stay this afternoon to work through some ideas?'

'Oh. Sorry, no, I won't be here. I've got an exhibition.'

'Oh. Fuck. I'll not have another chance for a week.'

'Couldn't Dorothy help?'

'Naw.' Cat didn't elaborate. Her feral gaze flicked over Bel's hair and bosom. 'What kind of exhibition? You in a competition?'

'No!' The denial was more vehement than it needed to be. 'I hate competitions. It's just – someone at Wigmore Hall.' Bel did not want this conversation at this moment. There was no reason to suppose that Cat knew or cared about pianists, even one as renowned as Mikhail Rakhin. And if Bel made it important, sod's law said the exhibition would go badly, and then she would look foolish.

'Competitions are fine if you win them,' said Cat as Bel rose and swung her bag over her shoulder. 'Good luck. Break a finger.'

Bel took in the leopard eyes once again. Everything was to be distrusted.

'Thanks,' she said, and departed.

The encounter stayed in her mind as she walked to Wigmore Street. It left her with a kind of pain that she didn't want to acknowledge. There'd been an afternoon back in December, the first anniversary of her teacher's funeral, when Dame Madeleine had summoned her services for a special session to help develop Cat's role as Isobel Gowdie, a Scottish farmer's wife famous for her confession of devil-worship in the form of orgiastic fantasies. The three of them had worked alone in the echoing studio, winter darkness falling outside, the old prima working the young to the limits of endurance. Cat might be a tough bitch, but she was also a dancer of spellbinding brilliance, one who yielded nothing and gave everything. Watching her driven – driving herself – to a sweat-rag of exhaustion, Bel felt she was witnessing genius hunting perfection. It was glorious, and terrible. It stank like lions.

She reached the doors of Wigmore Hall, and was annoyed by the rising of her heartbeat.

She informed the box-office of her presence, and received permission to enter the auditorium. A dozen or more people were seated at the front of the hall, below the piano that glowed alone and black upon the stage. As she walked down the aisle, one man turned, saw her, rose and thrust forward his fashioned stubble beard.

'Bella. Come through. Everybody, this is Bella Noel. The last of the Valkyries.'

Bel flashed a glare at him. Charles Peddie liked to treat her as a volcanic maverick requiring his governance as mentor and lion-tamer. She hoped he hadn't been talking too much rubbish about her. But the people around him didn't look fooled: she guessed they were summing her up the way people usually did – a bay mare, tall as a tree, mixed race therefore black, probably chippy, possibly psycho, approach with caution.

Professor Peddie was good at what he was good at: a shrewd and savvy Canadian who had turned a minor career as a musical academician into a major one as a college director and networker and programme maker, expert at dealing with sponsors and media. His enthusiasm for her musical talent was genuine, but she also knew he wanted his piece of her. Or in her. She'd twice kept him faithful to his professional duty, once drunk, once sober. She didn't resent it. The teacher-pupil interdict didn't apply: Anna was her teacher, not he. And at this moment he was someone on her side. 'Sit you a while, Bella. We'll be with you shortly.'

It felt like entering an examination. The memory of her first formal piano exam remained vivid: two strangers staring at the gawky nine-year-old in a murky Victorian room, the piano looming black, the keys as white and cold as mortuary slabs, and the click of a pen-top. Luckily, she had spotted a mark on the piano-lid to clean off with a licked tissue, so the piano immediately became her friend, and the rest was easy.

Grade five, that first exam, in order to tick a box. Grade eight a year later, for the sake of the certificate, but by then she was already moving beyond formal measurement.

An elegant woman among the men was looking intently at her, aiming that particular sort of smile that says You know me. She did, too, but couldn't place her without context. Not a teacher, nor a player. But, that was a thought – she checked round the other faces: were some of them also here to play for the maestro? Having prepared herself to be the centre of attention, it was deflating to think that she might be just part of a queue. Some comfort: there was only one other girl, very blonde, very beautiful, petite, immaculate, seeming semi-detached within the company, clicking text messages. In fact – Bel didn't know where it came from, some rogue spark of chatter, body-language, telepathy – she divined that the girl was Rakhin's daughter.

Bel was ambivalent about daughterhood.

Finally, she allowed herself to notice Mikhail Rakhin himself.

The maestro was sitting lazily in the front row, superb in cashmere, thick black hair flecked a little with grey, a man in the prime of his prime. He suddenly glanced at her, an electric touch of black Russian eyes. She stared back. There might be a thousand student pianists who would give everything except their arms for the approbation of this man. Instead of those thousand, she was the freak whom chance and Professor Peddie had brought before him.

His glance wasn't kind. Why should it be? How many other budding geniuses and promising talents did he get through in a week, a month, a year?

Fuck them. And fuck him. She worked for a living and she didn't need favours from anyone…

She heard Charles Peddie bringing the conversation round to her.

'Mikhail, are you okay to hear my prodigée now?' Either it was Charles's joke to conflate 'protégée' and 'prodigy' or he really thought it was a proper word. Bel disliked it either way. Anna had growled that musical prodigies were a nonsense, and she'd been one, so she should know.

The maestro waved one hand languidly. Charles turned and grinned menacingly through his beard at Bel. 'Good to go?'

TRACY MAYLATH

The Long Gestation of Madame Foo Foo

Synopsis

15-year-old Brian is deciding whether to kill himself though he reasons that he'll probably die anyway. If the conservative, Midwest American suburb in which he lives doesn't suffocate him, then Reagan's pressing the button most surely will. His family is baffled by him. Particularly his father, a religious, taciturn man who works in the aerospace industry and Brian's brother, Greg, 17, who postures as the kind of man Father expects his sons to be.

Plagued with barely suppressed thoughts that he thinks are sinful, Brian 'borrows' his mother's clothes when no one is around. The jocks at school bully him for what they guess is true. A gang beats him up guessing what Brian can't bear to admit to himself: that he's gay. Brian embarks on a half-hearted romance with his best friend Trace to try to prove to himself that he's the man his father wants him to be.

With the Cold War simmering in the back of his mind, Brian, like his mother, keeps returning to God to help him with his fears and the sub-conscious feelings that continue to press against the barrier he has pushed them behind. The thoughts threaten to finally come to the fore when Brian witnesses the casting out from the church of Ted, the leader of the youth group, when the church elders become suspicious of Ted's sexuality. His homophobic family becoming increasingly suspicious of his behaviour, Brian decides to hasten his own death and hang himself.

Father saves him from killing himself, but throws Brian out when he finds women's clothing in his room. It's a bittersweet emancipation. Brian can finally escape to New York, reflecting back on these years as a gestation period, and give birth to the drag queen he was destined to become: Madame Foo Foo.

Part 1: 1986

1
The Dark Butting Up Against the Light

Case Against

God
Dorothy Parker
Mother and Father
Greg (might go away to college)
Tracy (will lose best friend)
Chuck and Dean (could move or die)
Last minute regret
What if? (Things get better)

Case For

God
Nuclear bomb (probably kill us all anyway – so waste of a sin)
Mother and Father
Greg (he'll love being only child)
Tracy (Eileen could be a better best friend)
Chuck and Dean (probably won't move/die)
Thoughts(!)
What if? (Things don't get better)

The method, Father's Bugs Bunny tie, was all ready to go and now it was just a matter of whether I was going to put it to the test. I guess I was approaching it all kind of ass backwards, figuring out *how* to do it before I decided on *whether* to do it but that was just another case *for* even though I didn't write it down. Because it was a given that everything I did was, as Mother said, offbeat and her tone never sounded like she meant it as a compliment.

Mother's list of things that were offbeat, and therefore distasteful, was so long and labyrinthine, it would have been easier to break it down into categories with an example in each:

Clothing: wearing all black, hats on women
Television: anything on PBS, most foreign shows incl. Astroboy
Food: 'What's a meal that doesn't include meat when it's at home?'
Interior Decoration: bare spaces, neutral colours, shelves of books
Books: any book that didn't have a neon cover and a title that was a promise, 'Be More Confident in 7 Days!' with a photo of a toothy-bright author on the back
Misc: Sarcasm, gallows humour, the enjoyment of any weather that wasn't sunny

Writing my list in code was so she wouldn't cotton on if she happened upon it while I was still alive. Also because the thought of being dead and her trying to work out the 'Dorothy Parker', afforded me a tingle of superiority. Because obviously what I was alluding to was Parker's poem about suicide being harder than you'd think. Parker fell under Mother's heading of 'all those depressing books you read'.

One of the lists was supposed to, in quantity, outweigh the other list and that was going to give me the answer. And when they came out neck and neck, I flung the notebook away from me. Also because I'd heard that people just crying wolf had to think of reasons to die and real suicides had to think of reasons to live. So the fact that I was a hung jury in the judgement of my own existence, ratcheted up the depression dial from despair to desolation.

At least I could admire my handwriting, copperplate curlicues on and around each line of my college ruled notebook. But when I tore the sheet out from the metal spiral, I hated the ragged edge it left. So I scissored it off, plucked all the resulting confetti out of my orange shag-pile carpet and formed it into a tight ball. I threw that at my Astroboy garbage can and missed and then shoved the lists way deep under my mattress with the other things. I didn't want anyone to find it once I was gone or even if I wasn't gone, which I guessed I wouldn't be for a while anyway, at least until I could add something to the second list.

I supposed, to seal the deal, I could turn 'Thoughts(!)' into a heading and then add a list of specifics. But like Dorothy Parker, it was code. Mainly because if the parental units discovered even one of the 'Thoughts(!)', they'd haul me to the high school guidance counsellor without so much as a how d'ya do? And she'd want to fish around in my brain like my thoughts were the toys at the bottom of one of those claw machines at the arcade. She'd manipulate the joystick to hover the claw over the stuffed Care Bears and Garfields that lodged in my temporal lobe and, *kuh-ching*, drag them to the surface and examine them for the dead and depressing ideas they were.

Also, I didn't want subheadings of 'Thoughts(!)' because I didn't really know myself what they were. They were like news headlines, they festered insidious in my brain. The itch of them flared into anxiety in the night. Like the Cold War and Intermediate Nuclear Forces, I knew they were there but kept them behind a safety curtain in my subconscious. Because if I peeked behind that curtain, let alone lifted it up and let all the thoughts escape, I would have been rocking back and forth in my bedroom hitting my head against the Superman wallpaper beyond all capabilities of any guidance counsellor.

There were times when the assistance of the Magic 8 Ball was necessary. Like when I couldn't decide whether I had studied enough for a test, I'd ask it, 'am I going to pass this test?' And if it answered, 'Very Doubtful', I'd stick my tongue out at it and push aside the book I really wanted to be reading and crack open the book that I had to be reading. And just a few months ago, when the Space Shuttle Challenger was preparing to go up, I'd asked it, 'will all the astronauts return to Earth?' and it had answered, 'Don't Count On It'. So I put a lot of trust in it to decide my fate.

It was to hand in my nightstand drawer next to my solved Rubik's Cube and my mix tapes and my Walkman. I always warmed it up first, like a cop conducting a lie detector test to see how we were literally going to play ball.

'Am I ugly?' I asked it. I spun the ball around and around so that the icosahedronal die could pirouette in the blue liquid and come up trumps.

'Without a Doubt.' It said.

'Jesus Christ,' I strangled it a little before trying again. 'Does my life suck?'

'Signs Point to Yes.'

My stomach sort of flipped because it seemed like the hung jury might be inclined to become unhung and I might have to put Father's tie to work.

I shook it hard like a threat and whispered to it, 'should I kill myself?'

'Better Not Tell You Now.'

'Goddammit.' I hissed at it again, 'should I kill myself' and it answered 'Ask Again Later' so I fast bowled it toward my closet, returned to perusing my lists and told myself not to look at the word 'Thoughts(!)'.

I fixed my eyes instead on the word 'God', which got me thinking about whether God knew my thoughts and there I came jammed again between a thought and a hard place.

God was like Father. You'd be in your bedroom in the night with the door latched, tented under your comforter reading Salinger by flashlight and the next day Father would say, 'must be pretty tired today huh?

Staying up all night.' And God was presumably a couple of notches more omnipotent than Father so He must have known my 'Thoughts(!)'. But then if He were a loving God like Ted always said He was, then why would he make me think thoughts that were too awful to really think? And those thoughts about God and Father and omnipotence and loving versus wrathful tied my brain up in knots like it did when Mr Simpson was explaining about how to figure out what X equalled.

Speaking of knots, there was the hangman's one I'd been looping into the tie I borrowed from Father. It kept slipping loose so I'd given up and written the lists but I plucked it back up off the shag pile. It was supposed to look like the ones you see in history books, dangling from a gallows, but it wasn't working and I said 'goddamit' right on the beat of Mother's first rap on my bedroom door.

'Brian,' she said and I retied the knot. 'Brian,' she repeated. 'Brian,' third time unlucky, she raised her voice an octave like always. 'Brian,' I figured her knuckles must be getting sore. She rattled the knob on knock number five whacking up the volume to a range I would have been in trouble for, 'BRIAN'. Then she started her usual muttering, taking the Lord's name in vain, which I'd also get in trouble for. 'Jesus, Mary and Joseph, I swear to God, if you don't…. I don't know what in the heavens is the matter with you lately…I have told your father time and again to take the gosh darn lock off this door…crazy people putting a lock on a child's bedroom door.'

I refused to be waylaid by her nagging or the usual critique of the previous house owners or by the idiotic Bugs Bunny motif on Father's tie so I hummed 'Do You Really Want to Hurt Me' in my head as I took the knot for a spin. I drew it tight around my skinny wrist until my veins bulged. A 'goddammit' burst out of my mouth and Mother, like she always did with everything, made it about herself and Jesus.

'Don't you dare blaspheme at me, young man. You open this door right now you hear me?'

For once the blaspheming hadn't been about her. Not totally. It was because the stupid rabbit cartoon on Father's tie *was* distracting me. I'd been worrying that, when they cut down my stiff and distended body, the rabbit on the tie I'd chosen might be interpreted like a rune. I pictured them puzzling over what I was trying to say with the 'What's up, Doc?' Whether it was meant as a final, enigmatic message to the world when really it had just been the first tie that came to hand when I reached into his closet. Given his novelty neckwear collection stretched to command a foot and half of space next to his line of beige, button-down long-sleeve work shirts, my chances had been slim that I would have ended up with a plain one.

It could have been Star Wars or Mickey Mouse or 'Keep on Truckin'' or any of the others with which Father tried to prove to his colleagues that he was something other than a bastard. None of them were designed for the purpose to which I was about to put them. But I'd had to do a smash and grab raid on his closet while Father was at work and Mother was making dinner in the kitchen to the sounds of Phil Donahue bellowing on the TV in the living room.

As I'd examined my booty when I got back to my bedroom, slamming shut the door and flicking the lock, I couldn't help but giggle at the thought that this would be what they would find had strangled me. Mother always received more confirmation of her youngest's oddness whenever I laughed at the darkness of life butting up against the light. If I had known then that one day I would pay my bills by exploiting this chiaroscuro that life offers, I wouldn't have needed the tie, I would have known to just grit my teeth and wait out the gestation until I was truly born.

MAURICE McBRIDE

Six Days in Kashgar

Synopsis

The novel is a thriller set in the Xinjiang, the Uyghur *Region in northwest China; it is the story of a kidnapping that goes wrong, with repercussions that are felt across the world.*

It is partly inspired by the real events of the Achille Lauro *hijacking.*

When his younger brother is arrested in Kashgar, 17 year old Ismail Torre (together with his friends) decide to kidnap a Chinese tax inspector to force his brother's release. Unknown to them, the official is travelling with a visiting American Senator. They thus acquire a very significant hostage.

Refusing American assistance, the Chinese search for the kidnappers and make a heavy-handed attack on the location where they (incorrectly) believe them to be. The American authorities are appalled and put pressure on Beijing to negotiate the Senator's release, which they decline to do. Discussions go badly between the US and China, and the US Seventh Fleet is moved to station off the Chinese coast. A separate US rescue mission is prepared on the border of Kyrgyzstan.

Having no Intelligence assets in the area, the Americans request assistance from their allies and a British spy, Malone, is co-opted into the search.

Meanwhile a Uyghur separatist group, IMFET, becomes determined to find and capture the Senator, to further their own aims.

Malone is assisted by See Wing, a Chinese prostitute, and her friend, Mrs Zhonghang, who has observed the movements of Ismail Torre's friends going back and forth into the desert where they are holding the hostages.

The novel climaxes in the clash of Malone and See Wing, the kidnappers, IMFET, the Chinese military and the US rescue mission in caves at the edge of the desert – the Senator is liberated, and the US and China diplomatically agree that it never happened.

Six Days in Kashgar

1

1992

Her first thought was for her children.

The three thunderous knocks on the front door woke her and she was starting to rise from her sleeping mat when she heard the splintering crash of the door being broken in.

'*Mahmut,*' she hissed at her husband, shaking his shoulder. '*Mahmut! Wake up!*'

'What? What's happening?' he mumbled, fogged by sleep.

There was a heavy pounding of boots on the floorboards of their tiny hallway. Instinctively, she slid off the mat and lifted little Yusuf out of his cot, gathering him into her arms. Ismail, the four year old, was already sitting up. She beckoned him to her. Bright torch-beams skittered across the wall opposite

'*Police!*' shouted a voice from the hall, 'Get your hands in view!'

Suddenly there was a figure looming in the doorway, then another and another, spilling into the sleeping room. The torches were shone directly at her, at Mahmut, at her children, stabbing their eyes.

'Get your hands where we can see them!' bellowed the voice. It spoke in Mandarin. 'You! Woman! I need to see your hands!'

Reluctantly, she released her sons, lifting her hands.

'Get the light,' said the voice and someone found the switch and clicked it on. She blinked painfully, still holding her hands up. There were four men crowded into the small sleeping room. She could make out their black uniforms, the *Han* Chinese faces beneath their helmets, the heavy weapons aimed at her and her little family.

'You are Mahmut Torre?' snapped the voice, evidently the officer in charge.

'Yes,' said Mahmut. She glanced across at him. He had pulled himself into a kneeling position, hands raised above his head like a supplicant.

'Who are you?' demanded the officer, turning to her.

'I am his wife,' she said. Her eyes flicked down to her children, cowering beside her. The toddler started to whimper.

'Your name?'

'Meryem Torre,' she said quietly. She gestured towards little Yusuf. 'May I comfort my child?'

The man regarded her for a moment. He nodded. She reached out and wrapped both boys in her arms.

The officer turned to one of the other black-clad figures. 'Meryem Torre?'

'She's not on the list, no,' said the second man.

'Very well,' said the officer briskly. 'She stays here'. He addressed her husband again. '*You* – Mahmut Torre. You come with us.'

'Why?' she gasped, her anger getting the better of her terror. 'What has he done?'

'Your husband is under arrest for consorting with terrorists. We have witnesses who saw him, in a café in the Old City, three days ago.'

'What!' she blurted out. 'What are you talking about? *He* isn't a terrorist!'

'That remains to be seen,' said the officer.

'I had no idea – ' said Mahmut. 'I didn't know *who* they were. We were simply chatting.'

'About what?' said the officer.

'Sport . . . the price of animal feed. *Nothing*. I had never seen them before in my life. That can't be a crime?'

'What you have – or have not – done, will be established under questioning. Get up, *Turki*, and don't do anything foolish if you value your family's safety.'

Mahmut rose to his feet, holding his hands up.

'Where will you take him?' Meryem demanded. 'We have the right to know!'

'You have no rights,' said the officer flatly. 'He will be taken for questioning. It will be decided if he is to be charged; or, possibly, if he requires re-education.'

Re-education! The word sent a shiver through her. Everyone knew what *re-education* might mean, detention in some dreadful, distant prison camp. Men – especially Uyghur men – could disappear into those camps for ten, twenty, thirty years. Some were never heard of again.

'*No!*' she cried, throwing aside her caution. 'You cannot take him! He has done *nothing*. He is a husband and a father and —'

'Be quiet, woman! We can arrest females as easily as males. Who then would care for your children, huh?'

'*Hush*, Meryem,' said her husband softly. 'Do not make this worse than it has to be.'

'*Way Khodayim*,' breathed Meryem – *Oh God* – gasping at the terrible realisation. What could she do? There were guns pointed at her, at her little boys –

Were it not for the children . . .

No, *impossible.*

They were bundling Mahmut outside. She got up, lifting little Yusuf onto her hip, taking Ismail by the hand, and followed them out through the small hallway, across the courtyard, into the alley outside.

There was a pause while the van was unlocked and Mahmut turned:

'Meryem,' he called.

'Yes,' she said, edging forward.

'Wait for me – I will come back to you.'

'Of course,' she said.

'Now you must take care of my boys. Keep them safe.'

'Yes,' she said. *They are all I have left,* she thought.

'And Ismail?' he said, addressing the small figure beside her.

'Yes, father?'

'Take care of your mother and Yusuf. Be a good boy.'

'Yes, father.'

'That's enough,' snapped the officer in charge as the back door of the van swung open. In the dim light, Meryem could see seated figures inside, all men, all Uyghurs. Mahmut stepped up to join them. He turned to gaze at her as the door slammed shut.

A minute later the alleyway was empty except for Meryem and her sons.

Yusuf was whimpering in her arms. He looked up at her and mumbled:

'Daddy gone?'

'Yes, Daddy's gone,' she said.

'Back tomorrow?' he said softly.

'No,' said Ismail, staring forward into the darkness. 'Daddy's gone.'

2

2004

Malone had got to know Kashgar City during his first stint at the Archaeological Dig, and he was already familiar with Beijing from the time he had spent there as a student. But he didn't know anything about the vast Chinese interior, almost three thousand miles of it, between the two cities. You learn nothing about a place by flying over it. He wanted a closer look.

He decided to hitch a ride on a lorry travelling west.

He spent a day hunting around the transport hubs on the outskirts of Beijing, asking about for a vehicle bound for Kashgar. He finally found what he was looking for.

Mr Wang was a broad and stolid individual and not much given to conversation. He had difficulty, at first, understanding what Malone wanted. Why would anyone make such a journey, if he didn't need to? Malone explained that he wanted to see the country close up. Mr Wang consulted with his co-driver, Mr Li. Mr Li looked sceptical. Only when Malone mentioned money did the Chinese become interested and agree.

He stared out of the window as they passed the endless narrow shops, modern precincts, car showrooms, pagodas, grand new hotels, temples, faceless offices, sweat-shops and workshops.

When they finally cleared Beijing, Malone started to see things he had not expected; there were hillsides like Surrey, soft rolling slopes with low bushes rising up them. Further on, the landscape became dramatic where the rivers had cut through rocky outcrops, leaving majestic hanging valleys in their wake.

Occasionally, Mr Li would attempt conversation:

'So, Mr Malone, why do you go to Kashgar?' he asked.

'I work there,' replied Malone simply. 'For London University.'

'For a University,' repeated Li, in surprise. 'You are a teacher, yes?'

'No. I'm an Interpreter. On an Archaeological Dig.'

'An interpreter? What languages do you speak?' pressed Mr Li.

'Mandarin Chinese. English, of course; some Arabic, a little Spanish, bits of French.'

'So many!' said Mr Li, impressed. 'Tell me, is it very difficult to speak the English?'

Malone smiled despite himself. 'Not,' he said, 'if you are born there.'

At dusk, when they had had enough for the day, they pulled over and unrolled their sleeping bags. One man slept in the cab, while the others bedded down beneath the truck, avoiding the oil leaks.

On the third morning, some sixth sense alerted Malone that something was wrong. His warning antenna was twitching. He wondered if it was simply nerves – he was, after all, far from home and alone, travelling with strangers.

But, no, *something* was in the air. He couldn't put his finger on it, but it was there. He needed to remain alert.

That evening they stayed at a cheap hostel, and made their way down to the local night market, where they ate fried noodles and drank several bottles of *Tsingtao* beer.

'For a Westerner,' said Mr Li, 'someone like you, this is a hard journey. You must be used to softer travelling.'

Mr Wang was staring at him narrowly.

'Not really,' said Malone. He felt that he was being assessed. He took a swallow of his beer. 'You see, where I grew up, there are no *soft* men.'

'You are a British, no?'

'I'm from a part of Britain called Ulster.'

'Ulster,' said Mr Wang, rolling the strange word on his tongue. 'Tell me, is your country like this?' He gestured to encompass the night market, the steaming cauldrons of noodles beneath the strung cables of bulbs, the chickens on spits, the smoke rising up into the warm night air.

Malone was momentarily nonplussed by the question. A picture came to mind of the countryside around his native Londonderry; dry stone walls, the dripping hedges, the dank grey sky. He felt an unexpected pang of melancholy.

'No,' he said carefully. 'My country is nothing like this.'

The conversation lapsed, and Malone glanced at the two Chinese. He didn't trust them – but then, he reflected, he didn't really trust anyone. What if they were planning to rob him – and his uneasy feeling wasn't only imagination? If it came to it, he reckoned that he could handle them. Mr Wang looked strong, but slow. Mr Li was probably quicker, younger, maybe more dangerous. But no, he thought, he could deal with Mr Li.

Coming into Dunhuang on the fourth day, China surprised him again. Stretching out across the horizon, there were rolling red sand dunes. Camels were wandering on the road. Apart from the lettering on the road-signs, he might have thought himself on the edge of the Sahara.

His suspicions of his companions were hardening; there were unmistakable signs, little whispers out of his earshot, glances and barely concealed smirks when they thought he wasn't looking.

Ten hours of bone-jarring driving further on, they arrived on the surface of the moon, a vast landscape of small black stones. There wasn't a blade of grass or a tree in sight, and no birds in the sky. This was the fearsome Gobi Desert. At six in the morning, Malone's shirt was soaked through with sweat.

And now there was something else to notice. The faces of the people had changed. The women wore headscarves and brightly coloured clothes, with zigzag designs. These were the Uyghurs (pronounced *Wee-Ghurrs*), a Muslim Turkic people. They had entered the province of Xinjiang. For Malone, it didn't even feel Chinese anymore.

Here, Mr Wang turned for Korla, and along the northern road beside the great Taklamakan Desert, a 600 mile long burning basin of sandy nothing, bounded at the northern edge by the Tian Shan mountains, to the south by the Kunlun Shan range.

That night, Mr Li and Mr Wang barely spoke or looked at him as they ate and prepared for sleep. *Right*, thought Malone, no longer doubting his instincts, so *this* is it.

103

He bedded down beneath the truck, lying on his sleeping bag. He positioned himself close to the prop shaft, using it as a barrier from one side, so that anyone coming at him would have to approach from the outer edge of the truck.

Animals can sleep and listen – *with one ear open* – and Malone had trained himself to do the same. He had collected five big steel bolts, which he built into an unstable little pile and covered with a spare shirt, hoping that anyone moving would disturb them, giving him a moment's warning.

He slept.

Something woke him. He kept his eyes closed, senses stretching out into the darkness. He had heard a footstep, the creaking of a knee, someone breathing nearby.

There! The tiny *'clink'* of his little pyramid of bolts collapsing. A change in the air, the unmistakable smell of sweat, another human being close by. He opened his eyes. A shadowy figure was reaching towards him.

He shot out a hand and grasped Mr Li's wrist in a grip like a steel trap. Mr Li cried out in pain – and Malone lashed out with his boot, taking the Chinese on the side of his skull.

Malone jack-knifed his body and slithered out, still grasping Mr Li's wrist. He pulled sharply, hauling the Chinese out from under the truck. In the moonlight, he could see the knife in Mr Li's other hand – he stamped hard on the fingers and reached for the weapon. The Chinese rolled onto his back, so Malone planted a well-aimed kick into his groin. Mr Li doubled up in pain.

He was out of the fight.

Panting, Malone whirled round to face Mr Wang. The heavy-set Chinese was hesitating, his expression one of horrified uncertainty. In his hand he held a tyre iron, but loosely, without conviction. Malone glared at him, then spun the knife into the air and caught it one-handed.

'Well?' demanded Malone, shifting his weight from foot to foot. His blood was up. Part of him *wanted* the big Chinese to attack.

Mr Wang looked from Malone to his companion, writhing on the floor, then back to Malone. He shook his head. *No.*

'I warned you,' said Malone, grinning mirthlessly, 'There are no *soft men* where I come from.'

Mr Wang dropped the tyre iron.

'This is finished,' said Malone. 'You had better attend to your friend. I imagine he'll live.'

Mr Wang nodded.

'I'll keep the knife,' said Malone. 'And this never happened, right?'

In the morning, they resumed their journey westwards.

The only way to get from the east end of the Taklamakan to the west (and so to the mountain passes that lead to the outside world) is to choose one of two roads, one to the northern edge of the desert, one to the southern, at the foot of the mountains. For millennia, these roads had been travelled by merchants with their mules and their donkeys and their caravan trains and the roads existed for one reason; at the foot of the mountains, fed by rainfall off the upper slopes, there was occasional water to be found.

In the Taklamakan, water is more precious than gold.

And, at the western end of the desert, where these two ancient roads converge, stands Kashgar, the great teeming Oasis city, the gateway to China for two thousand years.

Malone alighted from the truck near the train station. He handed the knife back to Mr Li, nodded a farewell to Mr Wang.

He had arrived.

ROB PERRY

Dog

Synopsis

18-year-old germaphobe **Benjamin Glass** *wrestles with his fear of bacteria and a growing love for a dog that follows him home from the beach – a champion racing greyhound people call 'The Mighty Gary'.*

Benjamin finds a greyhound licking a dead whale on the beach. It follows him home.

The RSPCA won't take it. The dog warden doesn't work weekends.

Benjamin orders takeaway. The delivery driver, **Leonard**, *is interested in the dog.*

After a walk, Benjamin's neighbour says a strange man was hanging around.

Leonard returns. He says the dog is a champion racing dog. Benjamin mentions the strange man. Leonard says they are in danger.

They go to the snooker club. Threatening men beat Leonard up. Benjamin escapes.

Benjamin's caravan has been broken into. Leonard arrives. They head for his 'holiday home', stopping to see Benjamin's nan in hospital.

The 'holiday home' is a caravan in a field. Leonard says he needs to go shopping. While he's gone, Benjamin finds hidden food. He questions Leonard's motives.

In the morning Leonard wants to leave urgently. Gary's owners arrive. Leonard has betrayed Benjamin. They take Gary.

Benjamin steals Leonard's motorbike, goes home, gets a tent, goes to his nan. She's not in her room.

Benjamin rides to the track. He breaks into the kennels and finds Gary. He is discovered and locked in. Leonard arrives and frees him, then distracts the owners and Benjamin escapes. He rides to the woods to hide out. Gary follows.

Leonard finds them. He removes a tic from Gary's skin. He goes to get firewood. Benjamin thinks he hears Leonard returning, but it's the police.

They chase Benjamin into the middle of a Sunday-league football

*game. He urges Gary to run. He won't. They say his nan has died. He sits
down on the grass.*

One

Benjamin Glass was on his way to see a dead whale when the dog started
walking beside him on the sand.

'I'm going to see a dead whale,' he said out loud.

He didn't normally encourage dogs he didn't know, but this one
seemed sad. It was dragging a red lead and looking around.

'You probably shouldn't come,' he said to the dog. He said that because
he didn't know what a dog's grasp of death was – didn't know if it had the
tools to cope.

Benjamin found out about the whale in a newspaper at work. When his
supervisor Camille put him on tills, he used newspapers to obscure the
scanner so it wouldn't make him go blind or mutate his cells. She jabbed
her finger at a picture of the whale on one of the covers.

'You should go and see it,' she said, balled fist hovering over her heart.
'You should see how it makes you *feel*.'

Camille had already seen the whale because she had a complete and
intrinsic connection to all the animals of the earth.

'I wouldn't like that,' Benjamin said, spraying antibacterial cleaner
onto the conveyor belt.

'Maybe that's why you should go,' she said.

When they found the whale's body, Benjamin stood upwind and took
shallow breaths in case whatever killed it could leapfrog between species.
The dog sat down a few feet to his left. They stared at the soft pink whale
mechanism lightly dusted with sand. At its sad old eyes dried out in the
sun. Even though the whale didn't seem damaged, the sand underneath it
had turned red. Benjamin thought about blood slowing to a stop in veins
like water pipes.

'He's dead,' Benjamin said, pointing.

Benjamin imagined its internal organs all pressed up against each other
as gravity weighed down on its body out of water. He looked at the dog.

'Where's your owner?' he said.

The dog didn't acknowledge him, just sat gazing at the whale, blinking
and breathing. Its ribcage pressed out onto tiger-print fur. After a while the
dog walked over to the whale and licked the blubber.

'Fuck,' Benjamin said, glancing around to see if anyone had heard.
When the dog came back, it pressed its wet nose against his hand.

'Fucking hell,' he said again.

He inspected the new patch of moisture just above his knuckles. As he stared at the cluster of fine red hairs that had stuck to his skin, the dog watched him through distant, amber eyes. Slow blinks like it had just woken from a dream.

'I'm going to have to go home now,' Benjamin said.

Benjamin walked back with the saliva hand held out in front of him, the dog following loosely behind. Every now and then it stopped to sniff at vacant crab shells and bits of plastic washed up from the sea.

They made their way between the dunes along a sandy track that snaked up the side of the California Sands Caravan Park until they reached a hole in the mesh fence.

'I don't think you should come through here,' Benjamin said, pulling his sleeve down over the clean hand – the one the dog hadn't licked - for protection. The dog took a few steps forwards and shivered. 'If you get tetanus you'll get lock jaw. You won't be able to eat,' he said.

With that, he crouched through. He didn't turn back in case the dog got the wrong idea, just walked through the caravans, past a flat-screen TV box sagging in the rain and a bike frame with no wheels.

When he made it to the caravan the dog was behind him again with its tongue hanging out. It stared, glassy-eyed and mouth ajar as he slipped through the door and left it standing on the porch.

Inside he leant against the door frame and drew oxygen into his lungs. He washed his hands in the sink with anti-bacterial hand soap then slid off his jeans and put them in the washing machine. He crept back to the window and peered out between the curtains. The dog was sitting on the decking, watching the caravan park's flag wobble on its pole. Every now and then it closed its eyes for just longer than a blink and swayed. It turned back to look at Benjamin as he stepped away from the window and picked up the phone. He called directory enquiries to get the number for an animal welfare organisation and they put him through.

While he waited, Benjamin took two puffs of his inhaler. He held his breath until he felt light-headed and listened to faraway-sounding pop songs until a call centre specialist became available. Eventually a lady called Laura picked up the phone. She had a Welsh accent and a friendly voice.

'Hi, it's Benjamin Glass,' he said.

There were a few seconds of silence.

'Hi Benjamin Glass. What can I do for you?'

'I'm calling because there's a dog that won't stop following me,' he said.

Laura was silent.

'I found him on the beach by a dead whale which he licked. Then he followed me home,' Benjamin said.

'A dead whale?' Laura said.

Benjamin felt like she'd missed the point a little. It wasn't the whale on the decking.

'Yes. On the beach. Do you think he could be infected?'

Laura didn't answer, so Benjamin continued.

'I've had to take my inhaler,' he said.

After a brief pause, Laura came back on the line. 'Let's start with what sort of dog he is?' she said.

Benjamin thought about it. The dog was like other dogs, only his chest was deeper and his legs were longer.

'He looks like a racing bicycle,' he said.

'Right.'

'And he has an exciting coat like a tiger.'

'Okay.'

'Also, some of his ribs are poking out. Not in a hungry way. I think they always look like that, don't they?'

'Possibly?' Laura said. 'Do you think he's a greyhound?'

Benjamin considered it.

'Yes,' he said.

'Great, does he have a name tag on his collar?'

'I don't know. I'm trying not to touch him.'

'Where is he now?'

'I left him out on the decking.'

'Right. And he's still there?'

'I don't know. Shall I check?'

'If you could.'

Benjamin crawled to the door, stretching the cord as far as he could, speaking louder because the handset didn't quite reach the side of his head. He peered out through the letter box. The dog was looking directly at him through the slot. It licked its lips and shivered.

'I found him. He's still there,' Benjamin said. 'He's shivering now.'

'Is there a chance you could let him in?'

'No. None at all. He's a germ factory. I just need you to come and get him.'

Benjamin opened the curtain a crack. He felt bad for the dog because it was cold, but he didn't want it rubbing itself all over the soft furnishings and spreading its germs around the caravan.

'Is he injured?'

'No. Well, not really. His left eye is a bit bloodshot, I think. It's hard to tell from here. Is that what you mean?'

'Does he look like he's eaten recently?' Laura said.

Benjamin examined the dog though the window.

'Other than the rib thing?'

Laura didn't reply. Benjamin could hear the muffled sounds of her explaining what was going on to someone else.

'Benjamin, are you still there?'

'Yep. Still here.'

She hesitated.

'The problem is, we don't pick up healthy dogs.'

Benjamin heard the words, but they didn't seem to make sense. It wasn't his dog. He thought maybe he'd misheard so he asked Laura to repeat herself.

'We don't pick up healthy dogs, Benjamin,' she said again.

There was a long pause while Benjamin thought about things.

'Have you ever heard of Toxicara Canis, Laura?' he said eventually.

'I haven't, actually,' she said.

'It's a kind of parasite that lives in dog faeces. It's basically a horrendous worm that grows behind your eye and makes you go blind.' Benjamin waited a few seconds for impact. 'It can shut down your liver and lungs.'

On the other end of the line there was silence. The skin under Benjamin's chin was itching.

'There's a local dog warden I'm going to put you in touch with,' Laura said. 'I'm going to give you their number now.'

'Okay, good. Because I don't want to make a big deal out of this or anything, but he's already touched me a couple of times.'

'He's touched you?'

'Yes. On my hand.'

'Okay, I'm going to give you the number now–'

'Sorry Laura. It's once. It's actually only once.'

'What is?'

'The number of times he's touched me.'

A pause.

'Here's the telephone number Benjamin. It's–'

'I lied about how many times to make it sound worse. He's only touched me once.'

Laura read him the number and he wrote it down on an envelope with a pencil. His skin felt white hot.

'Do you have a neighbour that can help?' Laura said.

Benjamin didn't need people asking questions and snooping around. 'It's out of season,' he said. 'There's no one about.'

'Okay, the problem is that the dog warden is closed now. They're closed until Monday.'

'I can't really leave him on the balcony until Monday.'

'Not really.'

'Fuck,' Benjamin said, putting the phone down.

Outside, the wind was getting up, blades of grass all leaning over. Benjamin pulled on a pair of washing up gloves and went to the door. He opened it enough to peer out at the dog's slim body, shaking in the drizzle, tiny ripples running across its flesh. It squeezed its head into the gap.

'You're probably going to have to come in,' he said.

Two

Inside, the dog padded around, dragging its lead and smelling things. It was still shivering.

'You wouldn't feel the cold so much if you had a higher body fat percentage,' Benjamin said, following it into the kitchen. Its nails tapped on the lino as it walked over to one of the cupboards and licked a spot on the door.

'I'll have to clean that now,' Benjamin said.

The dog walked over to him and stood with its front paws very close together.

'I don't know why you're still cold,' Benjamin said. 'You're inside.'

With the marigolds for protection, he unclipped its lead. Then he leaned over and rubbed the thick bits of its back legs. Ran his hand along the bumps of its spine.

'Do you feel lost?' he said, putting his flat palm very carefully on its side. He felt the tremor of its heart pressing the ribs out and pumping blood around its body.

The dog walked over to the coffee table, brushing along the side of the sofa, then lowered its nose into a cold cup of tea with a dead moth blurring across its surface. Benjamin made a mental note of where it had touched. He wondered whether it was forced to drink seawater while it was lost. He poured the tea off the back steps into the grass.

'I'll get you something to drink,' he said, filling a salad bowl at the sink.

He put the bowl down in front of the dog and it drank for what felt like a long time. When it lifted its head there were tiny beads of water balanced in the fine hairs of its nose. Benjamin watched one of them fall into the fibres of the carpet.

'I'm going to put you in the bathroom,' he said. 'Because I can't think while you're touching everything and wandering around.' He shepherded it in with his arms by his sides. As he closed the bathroom door it watched him with quiet eyes.

'I honestly won't be long,' he said, hoping it wouldn't urinate.

Benjamin used disinfectant spray on the areas the dog had touched, pausing on a peach rug to spread his toes in the thick pile. He picked up a cushion and pressed his face into it, then shouted very loudly. He looked at his face in the mirror. It was red. He stood in silence.

'I'm okay,' he said to the dog through the bathroom door.

Camille had explained the importance of venting your negativity when a chicken packet split across the scales on Benjamin's till and dripped inside the circuitry. After he washed the pink chicken juice from his hands, she told him she liked to shout into her coat after a difficult shift. She said the flow of energy was constant and unerring and you had to give it somewhere to go. Like a river into the ocean.

Benjamin rolled the marigolds down his forearms and over his hands, then hung them on the edge of the sink. He tore a sheet from a notepad on the table and started a list of the places the dog had touched so far. Places like *the wall in the hallway, the sofa,* and *all over the carpet.*

The list was good. His memory was less reliable when he was worked up and it would stop him forgetting which items and areas the dog had smeared itself on. He carried the list to the bathroom and opened the door to find the dog standing on the bathmat, exactly as he'd left it.

'Sorry I shouted,' he said. 'I was just venting.' He used his hands to gesture 'venting' by waving them around his temples. As he spoke, the dog adjusted its ears like a different angle might decode what Benjamin was saying.

'I've got a list now though,' he said, waving the piece of paper. 'So I won't worry so much about you contaminating my things.'

The dog yawned.

'I'm going to have a bath,' Benjamin said.

Benjamin turned the taps on full, then folded his clothes and put them on the toilet seat. While the bathtub filled, he looked at his naked body in the mirror. His legs were covered in goose pimples. He automatically cupped his balls to check for lumps.

'You can lay down. If you want,' he said to the dog, motioning at the floor.

While the bath filled, the dog walked around in impractically small circles, then lowered itself into a sphinx-like pose, front legs straight out, back legs tucked under.

Benjamin stood in the water. As he crouched he felt the hot tide of cleanliness rise up and over his body. He slid down until it reached the bridge of his nose, blinked a few times, then completely submerged. He held his breath and watched his hair lifting up and away from his head, swaying like seaweed above him. The light on the tiles wobbled in neat, bright diagonals.

A long dark shape appeared above him, hovering over the surface of the water. He sat up but the dog stayed put a few inches from his face. The tag on its collar had a name written on it.

The Mighty Gary, it said.

JOSEPH PIERSON

Helen and the Fires

Synopsis

HELEN (30) sees a woman burn herself to death on the steps of the Bank of England, apparently in protest over the climate crisis. Her involvement with the cause leads her to question her own sense of guilt and the role of JEREMY, the man who sent her there that morning.

There have been other burnings, this was the third. Jeremy has been thrown out of a protest group, and rumour has it that he is spearheading his own, more extreme, organisation.

She researches the earlier suicides. ALISON, sixteen, down on the south coast; a physics student in Gillingham. Helen carries a lot of guilt and shame about the death of her mother, and the more Helen reads about the climate crisis, the more guilty she feels.

While visiting Alison's hometown, she discovers that Jeremy grew up on a farm nearby. The family home burned down in a fire started by environmental protesters. Is he really committed to the cause, or attempting to undermine it from within?

Helen confides in KATHERINE, a woman with whom she's been in love since she was sixteen. Katherine is killed and, inspired by Helen's writing, another young girl burns herself to death. Helen feels responsible for both women. She finds Jeremy at her flat and a can of petrol on the side. He confesses. He orchestrated these suicides; he had a hand in Katherine's death. Now it is time for Helen to do what he asked, to go back to the gallery in the middle of the night and burn herself to death.

She takes the petrol and heads into town. She sits in the empty gallery, then leaves. We are all responsible, she reasons, but killing herself solves nothing. She resolves to face the problems she has helped to create.

Helen and the Fires
1.
She shows her pass at security.

'It's late,' says Alberta, looking at the clock above the one-way glass.

'Stocktake,' says Helen.

She goes in through the loading bay, up the goods lift to level five. Back of house, a bank of lockers, an old couch the kids use on their breaks, the missing leg replaced with a stack of fashion magazines. The Members Room. Chairs up, lights down. A fine rain against the windows, the river beyond, St Pauls, a full moon on its shoulder. She does a count of the booze in the cage out back then heads upstairs to enter the numbers. She checks her emails, leaves a final out of office, logs off and takes a moment. A pair of her old shoes under the desk, a scribbled note to herself on an A5 clipboard, a diary she used to spend all day losing and finding again.

She walks across the main hall on zero into the tanks, huge semi-circular rooms of poured concrete. The first room is empty save a forklift half-extended, a pile of thick ropes on the ground. A square screen in the second room, suspended from the ceiling by tense steel wires, a film projected against the canvas. Dust swirls in the light.

A woman stands on the bluish frozen dirt, the sky a smothered white. Her thin arms dangle at her sides, a white muslin veil over her face. Crows caw sparely on the soundtrack. A woman in mourning. A woman who is dead already.

She showers in the disabled loo on level six, dries herself with a hand towel, twists water from her hair and spends a while sitting on the loo leaning under the hand-dryer. She gets dressed and steps out into the corridor. One of the other stalls opens and a man steps out in front of her. The homeless boy. He sees her, steps back into the stall and pulls the door towards himself.

'It's okay,' she says. She puts out a hand.

He reveals himself, head bowed.

'You hid again,' she says.

He's a kid, maybe twenty. Thick lips, obscene, like the mouth of a Caravaggio boy. Italian, dark. She takes him up to the restaurant, fetches the keys from the clearing station and unlocks the drinks fridge. He sits at a high stool looking out the window, at the Shard, at the red lights blinking on the apices of the cranes. She pops the cap with her lighter and puts a coke at his elbow. He shakes his head. 'No money.'

'Gratis,' she says.

She leaves him there, walks down to the landing and stands by the wide window, shoes dangling from her fingers. The atmosphere breaks. Lightning photographs the cityscape and a wave of rain moves towards the gallery. The temporary space beside her deinstalled, empty, save a single pink neon sign above the arched doorway. *The cause is beside the point.* On clear mornings, a precise trapezoid of light slides across these naked boards, the shape narrowing, distorting, as time shifts.

She waits for the rain to subside and heads into town. It's half four, August first, sun-up in an hour or so. It's chilly, she is not dressed for the hour, for the cold. Her beat leather boots clip on the flagstones, the city deserted. She crosses Millennium Bridge, up to St Paul's, where the naked blossom trees starkly diagram the uplit grey stone. Lamplight shafts through the trees. She heads up Queen Victoria Street, cold and clear-eyed, a vague but rich sense of premonition rinsed clear by the smell of summer rain.

Bank of England. Slender columns before the steps, the courtyard a stage. The protest will gather, filtering down Threadneedle Street, gathering at the junction. Lombard Street, the church, St Edmond the King. The high double doors are locked fast, the transom dim. She checks the time on her phone and seems to jolt clear of herself, to see herself standing here, head bowed, checking her phone. She resists the urge to look behind herself.

It's five in the morning and she concedes the obvious. There is no meeting here, it's too early, the boy lied. There is a flush of embarrassment, as though she's been duped. She sees herself in the bar, proud of herself, rocking gently on her heels as she reads to the room.

The boy touches her shoulder and takes her aside. We need people like you, he'd said. Writers, artists. Come to a meeting before the march...

What a peculiar lie, she thinks, though her dismissal feels forced, something hovers at the small of her back, a premonition, a presentiment.

A courtyard at the back, closed off with an iron railing, the padlock unfastened. Concrete flagstones, a step up to a small quad with grey pebbles on the ground and a knee-high privet border. A zinc-topped table in the middle, the rain on its surface suddenly lit white by a security light fixed to the wall, which bounces on as she approaches, a stage-light picking her out in the dimness of the yard. The courtyard bounded on two sides by grubby, turtle-coloured brickwork. She tilts an aluminium chair, flicks the seat with the blade of her hand, sits and lights a cigarette. A dying palm in a dull terracotta pot in one corner, its fronds brittle and frayed.

Bartek will wake up for work in an hour or so and find the note she's left. She could call him before he finds it, say something more conciliatory, or tell him to ignore the note, throw it away, or she could leave right now, get back before he wakes, tuck it in the bin and pretend she never wrote it, pretend she didn't stand in the kitchen at one in the morning, vacillating, enjoying the strange quietness of the flat so much she decided to leave it after all.

She closes her eyes and feels his anger tightening her stomach. This is not mine, she thinks, and the weight slides off. There is nothing to be done. She sits here, relaxed, tired, thoughtless for a while, the empty gallery in her heart and the thought of the quiet flat and an undisturbed run of clear days, with no responsibilities, opening broadly before her. She gives herself to the morning. It is easy, like a prayer. A pleasant, harmless sense of obscure purpose that makes it easy to delight in the novelty of the moment, the emptiness of the town, the quiet humility of the homeless kid. How pleasing it was to put a coke at his elbow and say the word *gratis*. Coincidences will slide into her life, gentle connections looping back on themselves, encouraging a sense of fate that she knows she is inventing but which is very seductive nonetheless. A strange, subtle balancing act, shifting her own psychology like the counters to a game she intuitively understands without knowing the rules.

The gate creaks. A young woman steps into the courtyard, stops and wrists her nose. Her mascara's run, she's been out in the rain, her thick orange jumper sodden, dripping, jeans frayed at the knees. She nods hello and Helen nods back. 'Are you here for the meeting?'

The girl shakes her head and steps onto the pebbles, pauses and looks down at her feet, at the noise they have made on the stones. She looks up. 'You have a cigarette?'

Helen gives her one and proffers a flame. The girl takes a lighter from her back pocket and lights her cigarette, the fuzzy, sour smell of homelessness hovering around her. She steps carefully over the stones, one foot placed neatly in front of the next, as though pacing out the area in her beat canvas shoes. Helen watches her. They look very much alike, the same age, the same build, a slight asymmetry at the corner of one eye that reminds Helen of her own reflection. A streak of foresight. Before she can phrase it, a pigeon alights from an alcove and plush-flutters between them, so low the girl ducks, laughs with a putter of smoke and walks over to the potted palm. She drops to her heels and drags something out from behind the pot, a bulky, knee-high object wrapped in a black bag. The girl carefully picks at the knot and then strips the bag off, revealing a rust-coloured jerry can. She stands and looks at the wall, her back to Helen. She kicks the can with the toe of her shoe. 'This is mine,' she says. An accent, south east Europe.

'Okay,' says Helen. A dream of doubles. She pinballs down the corridor, drunk, and opens the bathroom door to see herself sitting on the loo. Both selves shriek, terrified, and she sees them both from the doorway, a third self, disembodied. The perspective can't sustain, the dream rends, she wakes. The girl picks up the canister and brings it to the table, shoulder-sloped, leaning. It sloshes and cushes to the gravel and Helen sees the logo on one side, a sticker, the Shell symbol altered so that the rounded arches break into flames, the *s* dropped: *hell.*

'Protests this morning,' says the girl.

'Yes,' says Helen. 'You are going?'

The girl shakes her head. 'I won't make it. You buy me a coffee?'

Helen follows her back down Lombard Street, two paces behind. The girl pauses at St Mary Woolnorth, the gate padlocked closed, a blackboard chained to the railing with the porch café's opening times streaked by rain. The girl moves on and Helen follows her round to the Bank of England where the girl walks up the steps, sets the canister down and puts her arms out, smiling. A security guard under the arches on Threadneedle Street walks away from them towards the crossroads. The girl crouches by the canister, flips the lid and tilts the can forwards with one hand until cold bluish petrol puddles on the ground and splashes down the steps, unloosed.

'What are you doing?' says Helen.

'It is not petrol,' says the girl. 'It is water.' She lifts the can, puts a hand underneath it, raises it high then tilts it back towards herself. It splashes onto her head, pulling her dark hair forward in a sheet. The girl gasps, Helen takes the steps in two bounds as the girl lets her arm drop, the canister swaying to her side as she steps back and puts out a hand, fending Helen off. 'Back!' she spits.

Helen takes a step backwards, there is nothing beneath her foot and she awkwardly staggers down the stairs and rights herself, turning to see the girl take the lighter from her back pocket, set the canister on the ground and say, clearly, petrol on her lips, 'I am lighting myself on fire.'

An abrupt huffing sound hits Helen with a brief flash of warmth. The girl is aflame.

She turns on the spot, arms wide, fluttering blue flames rolling over her wrists. She staggers under the columns and palms the glass doors then turns and walks back towards the steps, dripping flames in her wake, small bluish pyramids fluttering on the concrete. Her eyes are closed. Her hair is falling. She drops to her knees and falls forward, sliding sideways down the steps, rolling over, once, the back of her hand slapping the concrete as Helen backs up, a hand at her naval, palm out, as though testing the heat, her movements clear and measured enough for her to later reassess her actions and flush with guilt when she asks herself, *And what were you doing?*

She slides her leather jacket from her shoulders and shakes it out. Something tugs at her arm, pulling her roughly back. The security guard unshawls her fluorescent coat and throws it over the girl in a roar of squashed flames. A shout – 'Back!' – and then a jet of foam spurts onto the girl, skewing the jacket like a slippery playing card, the flames repulsed, as a police officer walks steadily forwards, a thick jet of foam from the squat hose of a fire extinguisher pointing squarely at the mess, covering the concrete with sludge as the security guard stands squarely in front of Helen and tries to push her backwards, the woman's panic stupidly subdued by the dumb authority in her eyes. Helen backs away from her. The policeman stands two feet from the girl, the foam sputtering, spent, as a police car moves swiftly towards the junction so that Helen conflates the two, the policeman is both driving the car and standing in front of the burning girl. She reassembles the moment, she looks at the slow waving of the girl's arm, the skidded mess of foam across the concrete, flames flickering across her back. Whitish smoke lingers over the steps and around the columns like a ghostly chorus. The car stops abruptly at Corn Hill, the doors open and two officers jog to the policeman, who lays the spent canister at his feet and forearms his brow. His hat falls off and clonks to the concrete, exaggerating the strange quietness. He bends to pick it up. One of the officers breaks away and turns back to Helen and the security guard, who still has a hand on Helen's shoulder while she stares at the girl.

The security guard takes the policeman's hands in her own, wipes her hair from her face and, gasping, starts to explain what happened, what she saw. Helen backs up, she sits on Wellington's pedestal and lights a cigarette. Petrol. She smells her fingers. She is surprised to see her hands shaking. Her chest feels tight, it is hard to breathe. She tries to calm herself by assuming the panic is an affectation, she's exaggerating. She looks skyward. Two minutes, at most, since the girl tipped petrol over herself. Where did they all come from? The protests, she thinks. They were prepared.

A newspaper man in a red bib stands at the lights. The officer walks towards him, one hand up, the security guard following him two paces behind. People will gather. She looks at the huddled glow of the street-lights as they start to blink off, the morning whitening. A second siren starts up, escalating, parking on the Threadneedle Street side of the Bank, flanking the car. An ambulance. Helen scratches her cigarette dead on the sole of her boot. A fire engine stops at the end of Prince's Street. She is surrounded, the whole sudden trilogy of emergency services. She watches the driver slide from the cab and clap his visor down as one of the paramedics throws a fire blanket over the wet mess of the girl, kneels by the body and hands a space through the foam, trying to find a pulse.

JULIA RAMPEN

The Cocklers

Synopsis

Su Lyn is a modern-day slave in a crumbling English coastal town. But when she gets separated from the others, she has everything to play for.

Born in a small village in Fujian, China, Su Lyn follows her boyfriend to England, but they are duped into becoming debt slaves. Su Lyn persuades her boyfriend to run away, but before their planned rendezvous the cocklers disappear and she finds herself alone in a country she knows nothing about.

Meanwhile, in the same crumbling coastal town, retired cockler Harold mourns his wife, fights with his overbearing daughter and tries to ignore a memory scare.

Su Lyn learns how to fend for herself, but her new life is shattered when a debt collector arrives. While fleeing, she encounters Harold at his lowest moment. Su Lyn takes pity on him; Harold feels obliged to let her stay the night.

Harold is persuaded to let Su Lyn stay a little longer, and they start to get on, despite their differences. But when Harold's daughter discovers the situation she fears Harold is being exploited and tells him to call the police.

Su Lyn, fearing Margaret, makes plans to leave. Putting her ambitions on hold, she joins a new cockling gang so she can learn more about how to find her boyfriend.

One day, though, she realises they are staying out dangerously late in the hope of more profits. In desperation, she breaks the rule of staying invisible and calls Harold.

Drawing on all his memories of the tides, Harold manages to save Su Lyn, but later learns that other cocklers have drowned. The novel ends with both Harold and Su Lyn reeling with the tragedy, facing uncertain futures, but drawing comfort in their friendship and the beauty of the bay.

Su Lyn

When Boon Ho said, "he's here", Su Lyn knew there was only one person he could be talking about.

"Already?" She looked down in dismay. She'd raked like the others, bent down like the others, scooped up the shells that lay camouflaged in the sand like the others, and stuffed them into the plastic net. But her net was only half full.

"The minivan's there on the shore," Boon Ho said.

They were surrounded on all sides by a vast plain of sand. In the distance it looked smooth and brown, like unbaked clay, but under Su Lyn's boots it was uneven and oozing. It rose into dry ridges, and then cracked into channels filled with shadows and the silky glint of water.

A hazy green line marked the start of the land, where the silver minivan was already waiting. It seemed early to Su Lyn, but her opinion didn't matter. General Cockle was their alarm clock, their factory whistle, their temple bell.

And all around her, the cocklers were hoisting bulging orange plastic nets onto their shoulders. Last night they had been kind, friendly people sharing nicknames and flasks of tea, but now, anonymous in their waterproofs, they seemed like hardened soldiers.

"Don't panic," Boon Ho said. "Maybe he'll be in a good mood." She knew from the way he muttered it that he was lying.

The other cocklers were already walking. They formed a small caravan as they dragged their nets back towards shore. The wind worried at Su Lyn's jacket. It was relentless here – it moaned in her ear like an endless tannoy instruction she couldn't understand. Its gusts made her twitch, and then she felt the pain of the day's labour rip through her muscles. She wanted just to collapse on her dirty old mattress and sleep.

But General Cockle was early, and her net was only half full.

"He thinks I'm lazy," she said. "He hates lazy people. I've got even less than yesterday."

"It's your first week," Boon Ho said. "You're still getting used to it. Mention the hole in your glove. It's hard to rake when you have a blister." He cleared his throat. "Better not pull out the dictionary."

She'd thought she could learn as she worked. Gather words like shells. Then she'd picked up the rake and she was just muscles and nerves in a race against time. She felt the lump in her pocket. "I'd forgotten I even had it."

The huge sky made her feel very small. It was blue like an upside down sea, with foamy clouds crashing against the distant hills, and scales of sun and shadow twisting this way and that. Birds plunged into it, weeping like mourners. She didn't recognise any of their cries.

They trudged forward.

"You could take some of mine," Boon Ho said.

"Then he'll scream at both of us," she said.

Ahead of them, the cocklers kept marching. They were tough, but not as tough as General Cockle. He'd arrived in a shipping crate and raked and stamped and haggled his way up. He'd been slapped and sacked and made the butt of other people's jokes. He never smiled, except when he threatened you.

"I should have said more, my life," Boon Ho carried on, as if reading her thoughts. "Today I'll make sure he understands."

"He won't listen," she said. The only people General Cockle had to listen to were the ghosts, the English bosses who rang him up on his fancy mobile phone. And all they seemed to care about was how many nets he'd sold.

Boon Ho squeezed her hand through her glove. "I'll make him listen," he said.

Another promise. He made so many he should start a factory.

"From what the others say, this isn't a bad job," Boon Ho continued. "In a few years, we could actually make money."

She hated how cheerful he sounded. "Years?" she said. The end of the week seemed as far away as the horizon.

"I just meant once the debt is paid off."

"And the housing, and the food bill and everything else they take," she said. She was suddenly furious. "This is worse than the factory. At least we got paid."

He winced as if struck by the wind. But it was the truth. She'd listened to his stories for years, caught the bus to the city with them, cashed them in for a ticket to England. Now they were on the windy, neverending cold sand and he was still trying to peddle his fantasies.

"And there was no General Cockle," she said.

On the shore, a figure got out of the minivan and paced up and down. In the factory, one person showed you to your dorm, another person took you to the canteen, but here there was only General Cockle. He loomed over them like Boon Ho's drunken father - even when the minivan he organised dropped them off at the house he'd arranged for them to live in, there were the noodles he chose in the cupboard.

He breaks you like an animal, the cocklers had whispered as they served up the noodles the previous night. But it's easier that way. This is your life now.

It wasn't. It couldn't be. She stopped.

"He told me the net had to be full," she said. "I may as well leave now."

Boon Ho stared at her. "What do you mean?"

"I'll walk back. Follow the road. Tomorrow I'll go to a city."

There, she'd said it. Made it real.

Boon Ho was shaking his head. "Are you crazy?"

"I was crazy to come here." To listen to you, she almost added. She looked around at the strange landscape again. It might as well be a different planet.

"But, my life," he lowered his voice. "It's not just General Cockle. The snakeheads, the debt collectors. They'll come looking for you."

"The debt collectors only care about money," she said. There must be better bosses out there, better jobs for her to do. She could wash dishes, after all. She held up the net so the wind rattled the cockles. "I'm not paying them with this, am I?"

They stared at each other for a moment, long enough for her to notice the sand in his eyelashes and the cracks in his lips, and the lines of failure already appearing on his forehead.

"Give me the net," Boon Ho said eventually. "I'll take it to him. Maybe he will listen."

She shook her head. "He'll just shout."

If she backed down now, Boon Ho would convince himself that things would work out, like he always did. He was an unflagging optimist.

"We promised to look after each other," she said, and then, trying to keep the tremble out of her voice, she added: "Unless you prefer General Cockle."

Boon Ho sighed. He looked up at the vast sky and the distant shore before replying. For a few seconds the world teetered on its axis. But now he replied:

"Then in the morning, my life, we'll leave together. You still have enough cash for the bus fare?"

She nodded, her heart speeding up like a drum beat. Three crisp notes, still carefully wrapped and tucked under the mattress. But he might still change his mind.

"Come with me now," she said. "Leave the cockles. We can go this evening after everyone goes to bed."

Boon Ho shook his head. "That'll make him even more angry. We should give the nets back." He paused. "Maybe it's better if I do it."

She hesitated. It felt wrong to leave Boon Ho to face the wrath of General Cockle alone. But the drum beat inside her was getting louder, and General Cockle could so easily drown it out. As for Boon Ho, if she submitted to General Cockle's wrath, he would conclude with his usual cheerfulness that she was strong enough to bear it.

"Maybe it is better," she said. "You're right."

"Are you sure you know the way home?"

It took her a moment to realise what he meant. She had never considered the grubby cold house crammed with cocklers home.

"I'll be fine," she said. She would listen to the drum beat. He had said he would go with her to the city, and that was all that mattered. Now she had to make clear that she meant it. She gestured at the open expanse in front of them. "I'm not going to get lost, am I?"

He took the net from her. In his hooded black jacket, with each arm splayed, he looked like a penguin. She felt a sudden rush of affection for him.

"When I said crazy, I didn't mean..." she began. But the words didn't come. "I'm glad we're leaving this place together," she said finally.

He smiled like he understood. "I won't let you leave without me," he said, "See you at the house," and he began to walk across the sand towards the figure of General Cockle on the shore. Then he stopped and turned.

"Remember - stay invisible," he shouted.

That was the last time she saw him before the blue lights came.

Harold

The picture on the postcard was one of those old photographs of the town, girls in swirling skirts and red lipstick, boys with rolled up shirt sleeves, preserved in time by dark room chemicals. Harold turned it over. "Dear Gertie," the card began. "Wishing you a happy birthday from the USA. Found this gem at the bottom of my stationary drawer."

Oh bugger. Another one who didn't know. Another one he would have to write to. It was surprising how bad news failed to spread. He'd thought they all knew by now, but then, Gertie was very good at maintaining all kinds of distant friends. She would spend evenings at her bureau, carefully distilling their lives into letter form. "Dear Susie. Please send me her letters." No, he couldn't bring himself to write that yet.

He stood up and wandered into the living room. The tweedy light fell through the window, illuminating the carefully ordered book shelves, the photograph frames. Did Susie ever come to visit? Was she the American Gertie once brought back from church? He remembered drinks on the balcony, the sacrilege of her mixing his single malt with coke. But it was too cold for that today: the glass door to the balcony remained firmly closed.

The bungalow was built on a hill, and through the glass he could see the whole of the garden below, in shades of rust ahead of autumn's approach, and, as the hill grew steeper, the roofs of the town, and beyond that, the milky surface of the bay. The tide was coming in: soon it would be a shimmer of grey, and after that, darkness.

This was the first of Gertie's birthdays where he hadn't needed to fuss around looking for a present, or find an excuse to pop out for the cake, which he would drive so very carefully back, and reveal after tea, a candle for each decade twinkling on the top. Last year, he'd got the dates mixed up, and Gertie had spent most of the evening testing him with questions. He'd been defensive and she'd been concerned and neither of them realised that it was her they needed to worry about.

Perhaps he should have invited Margaret round, to mark the occasion. She was unlikely to be busy. But she would almost certainly turn up with an inferior cake and insist on eating it and loudly cry, which would not do at all.

No – he had to accept it, Gertie's birthday was just a day like any other day now.

He crumpled up the card in his palm and dropped it in the waste paper basket. He'd work out what to say to Susie later. He pulled on his coat and let himself out of the house. There were leaves to rake, big soggy clumps of them. He started under the apple tree, and moved slowly down the garden as the light expired. By the beech hedge at the end, screened by its coppery leaves, he paused to listen to the sounds of the unseen street: a car sliding into a driveway, home from work, a woman calling for her cat: "Dimples, Dimples." Then a passerby, talking to himself in a strange language, who seemed quite mad, until he peered over the hedge and saw it was just a bloody foreigner talking on one of those bloody phones.

He turned around and began working his way back again. On the other side of the fence, Reggie O'Brien's grass was overgrown. It had been that way ever since he was carted off to a care home, but there were lights on in the house. The long lost son must be back from Australia. Harold shook the leaves off the rake and rested against it for a moment.

In the upstairs window of the O'Brien house, a blonde-haired boy appeared, nose pressed against the glass. An intruder, he thought, before realising it must be Reggie's grandson. It seemed only a few years ago that Reggie had come round excitedly with pictures of the newborn bairn. "You'll meet him soon," he'd said, but he never did.

The boy vanished.

The paving stones were speckled with rain. He put the rake in the garage and went back into the house.

It was half past four. If he wrote the letter now, he'd have time to send it before the post office closed. He could drive back the way Gertie loved, along the bay. He opened Gertie's bureau and sat down awkwardly with a piece of lined paper. His handwriting was so straggly these days – his teachers would have rapped him over the knuckles for joining up letters like this. But his teachers were safely six feet under. He wrote: "I am sorry to tell you that my wife Gertie passed away shortly after her last birthday. Thank you for your letter - it was a kind thought. All the best, Harold."

He folded it up and pushed it into the envelope. He wanted to get it out of his house as quickly as possible. He put on his hat and headed to the car.

GORDON SCOTT

Sins of the Fathers

Synposis

Sins of the Fathers, *a current, poignant crime thriller set in Belfast, tells the story of Cordelia, a Catholic Religious Sister and strong female protagonist who, due to the present ongoing clerical child sex abuse scandal, is experiencing a crisis of faith.*

Cordelia's once best friend, Reagan Kelly, has committed suicide, never having recovered from childhood sexual abuse.

Disgraced, defrocked, and imprisoned former priest, Gerard Finnegan, is freed under licence having served half of his three-year child molestation sentence. Cordelia arranges to meet him.

Unremorseful, Finnegan describes his activities as pastoral pleasure. He is a living, breathing, human malignancy and Cordelia must act as God's instrument against evil. As he kneels in prayer, she slits his throat and with his dying breath reveals the existence of a dossier containing details on clandestine paedophile clerics.

Cordelia retrieves the dossier and phones Mike Madagan, Reagan's former police partner, now a private investigator and part-time blues musician. Confessing to Finnegan's murder, she insists that he owes it to Reagan to investigate and expose the ecclesiastical conspiracy.

Madagan works alongside the murder squad lead detective in a hunt for the episcopal exterminator. (Madagan's private investigation jobs run concurrently and interweave with both the main plot and Cordelia's outreach duties.)

The slaughter of errant priests dominates news and social media. Why is the church refusing to comment? Is the abuse scandal endemic and does it travel to the church authority's higher echelons? Cordelia contests the seal of the confessional and refutes Catholicism's authority to absolve sin. Bishop Haggan becomes Cordelia's final target. Culpable for the duplicitous airbrushing of priestly debauchery, Haggan's role in a hierarchy of religious hypocrites cannot be excused. Cordelia injects him with a lethal dose of Fentanyl, leaves the dossier at his feet, and attempts her escape.

Sins of the Fathers (extract)

Into the dark we dance and sing, children of the night we bring,
on a spit to be impelled, sinners all must roast in hell.
Lakes of fire and red brimstone, the devil sits upon his throne,
with a trident he will prod, the same shall drink the wrath of God.
                                        The Manuscript Of Melancholy

Wednesday 4th December – evening
Jesus wants me for a sunbeam.

A coif frames my face, a virgin-white wimple covers my neck and chest, and a long, black veil drapes from the coif onto a dark tunic. My plain Jane features suit the dress code perfectly. This is not an angelic charade. Entering service seven years ago to begin a two-year postulancy, a test to determine my vocational fitness for life in a religious order, I passed with flying colours.

Yes, Jesus really did want me for a sunbeam.

Then, eighteen months as a novitiate and three years serving under a Religious Sister's temporary vows. Catherine Bennett is my christened name, Sister Cordelia my chosen name. Not having sworn solemn vows, I am not a nun, and I wear the habit only on hallowed occasions.

Tonight is a hallowed occasion. I'm paying an unofficial, unsanctioned pastoral visit to former Father, Gerard Finnegan. Disgraced, defrocked, and imprisoned, Finnegan was freed under licence having served half of his three-year child molestation sentence. I've had two phone conversations with him and he's agreed to meet me. He'll be expecting me to pray for him.

My accommodation is within a convent, yet I do not live a cloistered existence. My outreach duties include helping the poor and convalescing sick, assisting in care homes, aiding priests in parish duties as required, and running a female children's group. That's how I learned about Finnegan's release; the police are obliged to inform youth leaders of sex offenders in their locale.

I've previously reconnoitred Finnegan's small, detached, Antrim Road bungalow and am confident of clandestine entry and exit. The convent provides me with transport and I park my rusty Nissan Micra in a tree-sheltered driveway, survey the surroundings, and walk slowly up the path. I bang a hefty brass knocker and as the door swings open, I baulk on seeing a heavy-set, fiftyish man with bald head, yellowing beard, and moist red lips.

'Sister Cordelia,' he says. 'Please, come in.'

127

He leads the way into a dark, dingy, living area and points to a seat.

'I appreciate the visit,' he says, 'however, my sins are already forgiven. The Bishop has heard my confession and I've received absolution.'

So that makes it alright then; Catholicism employing a convenient scripture interpretation to bestow sin-forgiving power on priests. As you'll have guessed, I'm experiencing a crisis of faith, not in God, but in the duplicitous nature of organised religion.

'Of course,' I say. 'Nevertheless, I'm sure you could use a little spiritual support.'

'Any support is welcome these days,' he says.

'How do you spend your time?' I ask.

'Walking, reading, TV, computer; all devoid of human interaction.'

'No family connections?'

'Family, former friends, and the church; I encounter a leper's treatment on all fronts.'

'You expected a red carpet?'

'Sister Cordelia,' he says, eyeballing me. 'You're here to patronise?'

'I'm sorry,' I say. 'Can I help in any practical way? Shopping or housework maybe?'

'I prefer to fend for myself. Tell me about St Joseph's.'

'Your old parish is thriving again. Some younger members stopped attending after the scandal but two youth groups are now flourishing.'

'The joys of youth,' he says dreamily. 'And Father Cuthbert?'

'The congregation love him. He's a thoughtful priest and a good man.'

'Yes, thoughtful and good. He and I are old acquaintances you know.'

I try deciphering Finnegan's facial expression. Old acquaintances. He's definitely hiding something.

'I help him with Sunday Mass preparations,' I say.

'I miss St Joseph's greatly; it was my life for so long.'

'Why not move away? Why stay where you're not wanted?'

'Although I'm an outcast, this is my home.'

'Did you receive counselling?'

'Counselling?' he asks, puzzled.

'Is your illness cured?'

'Only the sick need cured.'

'You still have carnal feelings for young boys?'

'Maybe, dear Sister Cordelia, maybe young boys have carnal feelings for me.'

I shake my head in disgust. 'Your unspeakable sin will never be forgiven.'

'No morality lectures, please. I'm tired listening to moral high-ground speeches, particularly when spewed from the mouths of hypocritical priests guilty of the same acts that put me behind bars.'

'You're aware of other paedophile priests?'

'Ahh,' he says, smirking. 'You've at last managed to utter the "P" word.'

'How else can your crime be defined?' I ask.

'Pastoral pleasure, a perk of the job, and only a crime in the eyes of the law.'

'Pastoral pleasure?' I say, aghast.

'I've shocked you, Sister?'

'Your absolution is meaningless.'

'I'll repent when the church repents. The cover-up stretches to the highest echelons and yes, I've gathered a dossier on paedophile clerics in our diocese, clerics who administer Mass to congregations ignorant of their pious pastor's extra-curricular activity.'

'Why the dossier?'

'I plan to have Bishop Haggan restore my stipend; otherwise, a few sleazy ecclesiastical secrets will hit the headlines. I've got names, places, and dates going back years.'

'The victims have remained silent?'

'It's what happens. The little boys are now adults with families and careers; they fear the stigma associated with exposure. Besides, most so-called victims probably enjoyed it.'

I feel nauseous, his depraved, callous, inhuman portrayal of child sex abuse causing my mind to spin.

'Did you ever possess a genuine calling to the church?' I ask. 'Was your priesthood simply a gateway into preying on children?'

'I was once God's chosen and the church led me astray. You still wish to pray for me, Sister?'

Any lingering doubt clouding my course of action has dissipated. Finnegan has debased religion. He is an abhorrence, a living, breathing, human malignancy and his contagion must be erased. I swallow hard before answering.

'On your knees,' I say.

He obeys, his kneeling side-profile a picture of penitence.

'Close your eyes and consider your sin,' I say.

Inside my tunic pocket, I grasp the small Karambit knife. Designed to resemble a Tiger's claw, it fits my grip effortlessly. A clock's tick punctuates the passing seconds as Finnegan mouths a silent prayer.

'Lord,' I pray aloud, 'this man is a sinner. You know the depth of his evil ways.'

129

Finnegan whimpers, a tremor running through his body. His eyes remain closed and his hands are clasped against his chin. It's as if he knows his fate.

I continue, my palms sweating. 'As penance, he deserves to forfeit his earthly life and suffer the full extent of your wrath.'

'Dear God', he murmurs. 'Please forgive me.'

I slip the knife from my tunic and recite Nahum 1, verses 2 and 3.

'The Lord is a jealous and avenging God; the Lord is avenging and wrathful; the Lord takes vengeance on his adversaries and keeps wrath for his enemies. The Lord is slow to anger and great in power, and the Lord will by no means clear the guilty. His way is in whirlwind and storm, and the clouds are the dust of his feet.'

I execute a back-handed swipe and the three-inch curved blade arcs through the air, lacerating Finnegan's neck, slicing muscle, sinew, and jugular vein. Spurting blood spatters walls and sprays furniture, the manifest effect of a ruptured, depressurised cardiovascular system.

He clutches his throat and lies prostrate, crimson liquid cascading between his fingers as the blood tide refuses to be stemmed. He locks his gaze on me, his lips forming a smile. I lean over him as he tries to talk.

'Th...thank you,' he says.

'You're welcome,' I say. 'The pleasure was all mine.'

The jets of escaping blood turn sluggish.

'The evidence,' he whispers.

'Where is it?' I ask.

He points feebly at a door. 'Punish them.'

I nod. 'It will be done.'

'The last rites,' he says.

'Females are not granted power to deliver rites.'

As his breathing becomes laboured, I concede a few contrite words.

'The Lord have mercy on your soul,' I say.

Soon, his eyes glaze and I sit for a long time, quietly contemplating the death of a defrocked priest.

Do you feel misplaced pity for the late Father Finnegan? Please, just remember his offences; he was a paedophile who used his priesthood to groom and prey on the vulnerable. His sexual depravity has scarred the minds of countless children and your pity should be reserved for the victims of his evil deeds.

Finnegan was convicted for his crimes, yet others are living a saintly pretence, conducting daily church duties with impunity whilst remaining at liberty to abuse again. Our church leaders have covered up the clergy's sins, sins which must be exposed. Stay with me as we travel along retribution road. I promise, the journey will not disappoint.

I think about Reagan Kelly and the vile debasement suffered at the hands of her paedophile father. At face value, a family man, an upright citizen, and a sanctimonious Catholic deacon, by his debauchery he betrayed the trust of his only child. Reagan was my best friend until I found religion and she found a career in the police service. Wreaking revenge on many sexual predators before she died, in her memory, I intend to do the same. I'll tell Reagan's story later.

I roll on latex gloves, walk to Finnegan's bedroom, and find the dossier lying on a bedside cabinet. The contents will provide interesting night-time reading and supply vital intelligence, ammunition for my war on an ecclesiastical conspiracy, a conspiracy designed to conceal the truth.

At the priest's feet, I light a candle and place my hand-printed message in front. It reads, 'Retribution for Reagan' and quotes Nahum 1, 2-3. Finally, I bend Finnegan's arms across his chest, enfold his hands together in prayer, and using my phone, capture several posterity snapshots. Casting a validating glance at the carnage scene, I remove my coif, wimple, and tunic, beneath which I'm wearing charity shop casual clothes, and bundle the soiled garments into a black plastic bin liner. Shutting the door behind me, I peel off the gloves and depart.

Occupying a small apartment inside the convent, I time my return to coincide with Compline, a period when all nuns attend chapel for evening prayer before retiring; consequently, I'm not unduly concerned about meeting anyone as I descend to the convent's basement to incinerate my blood-stained attire. There will be numerous suspects for Gerard Finnegan's murder and a devout, holy order Religious Sister should be last on any list.

I sit on my single, metal-framed bed and begin reading the hand-written dossier. A page on each offender documents names, addresses, incident dates, and background information on victims. I take frequent breaks to digest the heart-rending chronicle of debaucherous acts and am disappointed, disillusioned, and dismayed at the named and shamed trans-gressors. Among the five culprits is Father Damian Cuthbert.

At 1.00 a.m., I close the file and decide to report Finnegan's punishment. Activating my anonymous prepaid phone, I dial Mike Madagan's number. Ex-Detective Inspector Madagan was once Reagan's police partner and is now a private investigator. It is fitting for him to be the first to know.

'Wakey, wakey, Inspector,' I say as he picks up.

'I'm no longer a cop,' he says groggily. 'Dial 999.'

'This case requires your expertise.'

'What case, and why call me at such an ungodly hour? Who are you?'

'Names are not important. I guarantee it'll be more exciting than your present work schedule; snooping around corners and hiding in shop doorways to spot adulterers must be pretty mind-numbing. Surely you'd welcome a real investigation?'

'Okay,' he says, sighing. 'A sick joke. Who put you up to it?'

'A world full of evil is no joke, detective.'

'You've read too many fairy tales, lady. Go get a life.'

'I've got one, and my vocation is retribution. Retribution for Reagan.'

'Reagan Kelly?' he asks.

'She was the victim of a bible-thumping paedophile and it destroyed her. My first target was a former priest named Gerard Finnegan; he's decomposing on the floor of his Antrim Road home. The police can find him on the sex offender's register.'

'This is not my business.'

'I'm making it your business and you owe it to Reagan. The church is infested with Finnegan's and a hypocritical religious hierarchy is attempting to airbrush it. We need to unmask these crimes, Madagan. We'll get to know each other better next time and be assured, there will be a next time. I intend communicating only with you.'

I switch off the phone, snuggle under the bed-covers, and fall into a sound sleep, dreaming of the next clerical charlatan to face, by my heavenly hand, God's wrath.

MICHELLE SHINN

The Recollective

Synopsis

Zachary Weaver *is a Recollective, an expert in memory manipulation and retrieval. His outgoing twin sister* **Jasmine** *was his best friend, supporting him until she was posted overseas. Recently promoted at the Tilder Institute for Memory Research, Zach craves his family's approval.*

When a mysterious girl is discovered who has no idea of who she is, Zach must help her find her missing memories. She is suffering with Tilder's Disorder, an aggressive, early onset of Alzheimer's disease, experienced by people who have been genetically modified.

While he is helping her, Zach discovers false memories have been implanted in her brain, hindering her recovery.

Aided by forthright journalist **Jin Chang**, *Zach uncovers a conspiracy at the institute. They are receiving funding from an organisation in direct opposition to them,* **Religion First**. *Religion First is gaining political popularity, publicly shunning the scientific approach of the institute as it conflicts with their values.*

When the girl is named as **Laurel Sanchez**, *Religion First claim she is part of their commune, demanding her return. Zach vows to find the truth, discovering they have been experimenting on vulnerable people. They hope to influence society to follow their radical ideology by implanting false memories.*

Just as Zach is on the cusp of exposing the conspiracy, his uncle reveals Zach deleted his own memories. After a tragic accident that Zach believes was his fault, Jasmine succumbed to Tilder's Disorder. Grief stricken, Zach faces a crisis of confidence. Is science the answer to the world's problems?

Zach exposes Religion First's true motives and their leader is arrested. Laurel's real memories are successfully restored. Zach has fallen for Jin, and wins a promotion at the Institute. While professionally he has succeeded, personally he is left with the agonising loss of his twin sister.

Prologue

Night.

She walks in the middle of a road, barefoot. Stumbles, nearly falls.

There are no streetlights, no houses, no cars.

She can make out the tall grasses either side, the trees, the hills. The hills loom over her; so colossal they could be mountains, their peaks swallowed by the darkness. The road disappears into inky black.

She stops. Turns to look behind. More of the same. She walks onward.

All is quiet, her breathing loud, coming short and fast. The only other sound is the gentle hum of insects, whispering to each other, watching her progress.

A biting wind blows the tops of the trees, and they wave. It finds her, poorly attired, in just a thin smock. Wraps itself around her, nipping.

Her left foot smarts with each step, and she winces. Stops to investigate. She sits down heavy on the tarmac; it feels cold against her skin. Bending her leg, she brings her foot towards her. Runs her fingers along the sole, it's gritty, and she clears away the gravel and dust from the road. There. Near her big toe. A cut. Not too deep. Sore to the touch. She inhales a shaky breath.

Her head is pounding. She runs her fingers through her hair, exploring. It's greasy at the roots, but then matted, knotty. What's that? The lump is hard, round. Halfway down her skull. The hair around it feels sticky.

She feels like she is waking from a long sleep. Beginning to form thoughts again. Searching for reason. Searching for anything. Because there's a problem. The problem is she can't remember. She can't remember where she is. How she got here.

Worse than that. She can't even remember her own name.

Her heart pounds faster. Time to get up. Time to get moving.

Pushing herself upright, she concentrates on keeping her balance.

Deep in the darkness a glow begins to form.

Headlights.

Chapter 1

The sky was defiant, a blue tropical ocean, with a wisp of cloud so fine it seemed they might have a day's reprieve from the usual storms. The sun shone kindly on the day of the official opening of the new institute. Thought to have cost millions to construct, the building was four stories high, with floor to ceiling glass on every level, and curved walls that seemed to undulate gently.

The event had been planned to take place in the vast, open reception area on the ground floor but on account of the good weather, the glass doors had been thrown open and the guests had spilled out onto the patio, despite the intensity of the sun. Scientists, psychologists, doctors, the very best in their field, along with their families and the press, had all been brought together to celebrate the anticipated success of the new centre.

Zach stood in the shadows, trying to blend in, unaware that his messy blonde hair stood out like a beacon next to the rich ebony pillar. At six foot five, it was hard for him to go unnoticed, and he recalled how his Aunt Sheila had always told him to stand up straight and stop hunching. Zach had relieved one of the waiters of a glass of champagne as they'd hurried past, and he brought it to his lips, feeling the pleasant fizz of the bubbles on his tongue. A welcome distraction, it gave him something to do with his hands while he observed the reception, checking his phone intermittently. No sign of Seb yet. He pulled at the tie he'd bought, feeling restricted.

Despite his reluctance to attend, he had to admit that marketing had done an impressive job. No detail had been overlooked. Banners suspended on thick wires hung from the cathedral height ceiling proudly displaying the values of the centre, 'Collaboration,' 'Progression,' 'Transparency'. In one corner, a 3D hologram of Greta Tilder talked animatedly about the history of the institute, explaining why she founded it. Speaking to the hologram prompted her to become interactive, giving you a tour of the areas of the facility that were open to the public today.

Waiters circulated with extravagant looking canapés, tiny morsels of specially imported beef, a rare treat these days, along with rambutan-flavoured ice cream designed so it didn't melt in the heat. Unsurprisingly, the brain shaped fruit flavoured jellies didn't seem to be going down quite so well. When another waiter approached him with an untouched tray, Zach suggested he should try with the kids, he was sure they'd get a kick out of them.

'Did you notice?' He hadn't seen Clove approach and he jumped a little when he heard her voice near his ear.

'Notice what?' The glass in her hand, misty eyes and lack of regard for his personal space indicated she had already taken advantage of the free bar.

'The lack of verbal abuse, no chanting.' She motioned outside.

She was right. The usual rabble were conspicuously absent.

'Do you think Mayer paid them off? Had them murdered?' She grinned at him mischievously.

'I think you've had too much champagne,' he said.

'Oh come on, it's a celebration. Not often we get to have a drink in the afternoon at work.'

'I can see why.'

She rolled her eyes. 'Seriously though, what do you think happened?'

'With what?'

'The protestors.'

Zach considered it for a moment. 'Maybe they just came to an agreement, I don't know?'

Maybe,' said Clove. She didn't look convinced.

They stood together in a comfortable silence, observing the people milling around outside on the patio, polite smiles and handshakes. Soft notes floated over from a string quartet.

'How are you feeling?' she asked, taking a sip of champagne.

'Ok.'

She looked at him, eyebrow raised.

'Maybe a bit nervous,' he admitted. He glanced over at the stage that had been set up next to the reception area, the podium, the microphone. He felt the beginnings of a headache.

'You'll be great.' She smiled. 'Are you coming outside for a bit?'

'Sure.'

As Zach followed Clove outside, he wondered how much longer he'd be able to rely on her. She had been his Personal Assistant for three years now. Fiercely intelligent, she'd dropped out of university due to an unexpected pregnancy. She didn't talk about the father much, but from what she'd said Zach had been able to figure out he'd not given her much support. She still lived at home with her parents, relied heavily on them for childcare. Sadie was five now, and Clove had returned to her studies. She was doing well. So well it wouldn't be long before she'd graduate, move on to a research position in the institute. It made him feel sad. She was one of the few people he felt comfortable around, that he could be himself with. It was because she reminded him so much of his sister.

Bright sunlight blinded him and he retrieved his sunglasses from his pocket, slipping them on. It was like walking into an oven. Beads of sweat prickled at the back of his neck. He took off his jacket, folding it over his arm.

Beyond the patio, perfectly manicured lawns cascaded down a gentle slope. The sprinklers were on and kids ducked in and out of the spray, carefree and giggling, arms spread wide, like aeroplanes. They've got the right idea, thought Zach.

The gardens were an oasis of calm, much needed for the patients they treated and a welcome respite for doctors too. Green spaces were neatly arranged into a patchwork of squares, interwoven with gravel paths lined with pristine hedges. At the centre of each square was a different feature, a perfectly planted flowerbed, a carefully crafted topiary. In the far corner of the grounds was a maze, with a sculpture of a human brain in the centre.

They deposited their glasses on the tray of a passing waiter, helping themselves to fresh ones. Might help the nerves, thought Zach. Clove was scanning the crowd.

He glanced at his phone again. Nothing. 'What time are they due?' he said.

'Any minute,' she replied, eyes fixed on the mingling people. She turned. 'Any word from your uncle?'

'Not yet. Knowing him he's forgotten.' He tried to make his tone light.

'I'm sure you're right.' She averted her eyes. Her phone buzzed. 'They're here,' she smiled. 'Let me just go find them.'

'Sure.'

He took a sip of his drink, letting his gaze wander beyond the gardens to where the protestors usually gathered, near the fence. Not that he could make out much of the fence. While everything inside the centre was perfectly controlled, outside the natural landscape flourished, the tropical climate encouraging wild growth. Trees towered, leaves were the size of tables and grasses grew past waist height. He and Jazz used to play hide and seek in the grasses when they were kids, before the accident. There was one time, not long before it happened, when he couldn't find her, that panicky feeling in his chest, the headache, and then, a flash of pink from the ribbon in her hair-

'Dr Weaver?'

He blinked the memory away, turning towards the woman who addressed him. She was striking. Half of her head had been shaved, covered with an intricate floral tattoo. Shiny dark hair tumbled over the other side down to her waist. She wore a silver earring that started at the top of her ear, trailing to a chain that looped her earlobe. Her lips were stained bright red.

'Yes – sorry, I was miles away.'

'Jin Chang,' she extended her hand.

'Zach, nice to meet you.'

'And you.' She tucked her hair behind her ear, looking up at him. 'So. This is all very impressive,' she said, gesturing to the reception.

'Sure.'

'Quite an investment I'd imagine.'

He shrugged. 'I've not been involved in arranging it.'

'Of course.'

He took a sip of his champagne.

'I'm sorry, I should have congratulated you.' She touched his arm lightly and he caught the zesty scent of her perfume, what was that, oranges? He realised she was still speaking. 'How do you feel about your new position? Lots of pressure I imagine?'

'I guess so, sure.' He rubbed the skin in-between his eyes with his forefinger, taking a step back. Surely she must realise he'd seen the pink band on her wrist, knew she was press. He wanted to make his excuses and leave, but there was something about her that compelled him to stay.

'What do you think–' she started.

'We're back!' Clove announced, family in tow.

'Clove,' Zach was relieved. Jin Chang was unsettling. He introduced Clove, melting into the background as they engaged in conversation.

He checked his phone again. A message from Uncle Seb.

Sorry Zach. Can't make it this time.

His head pounded.

The audience had gathered in front of the stage. An expectant hush had fallen. Zach stood with Clove and her family, waiting for Mayer's entrance.

Suddenly, a murmur rippled through the crowd. What he lacked in stature, Mayer made up for in charisma, he swept across the reception area, nodding and shaking hands. The attendees parted to allow him through. Dressed impeccably in an expensively tailored navy blue suit, he mounted the stage energetically with a small jump.

He greeted the audience with a smile. His silver hair seemed even more elaborately coiffed than normal, his skin a deeper shade of bronze.

'Good afternoon,' his voice was smooth as treacle; he spoke in an American accent with a twang that betrayed his European heritage.

'Welcome friends, colleagues, esteemed members of the press, to the opening of this building, the Tilder Institute for memory research.'

Zach joined the applause from the audience, and Mayer clasped his hands together as if in prayer.

'Thank you. I thank you for your participation today.' He rested his hands on the podium in front of him, his dark intelligent eyes scanning the room.

'My name is Dr. Lukas Mayer, and I am deeply honoured to have been appointed the Managing Director of this centre. Today represents a new beginning, a new vision for our future. A future where we can finally overcome Tilder's Disorder, the devastating condition that affects so many of our society. A future where science can be the victor, demonstrate the value we add to the world. This building and every one of you here is representative of the hope–'

He shook his head, raising his voice emphatically. 'No, the *confidence* I have that we *will* be successful.'

Applause broke out in the room, louder than before, and lasting for several minutes. Mayer smiled, nodding in appreciation.

'Now, on to the building itself. I have worked carefully with the architect to achieve what I hope is a reflection of the values of our organisation.

'Firstly, transparency. Look around and you will no doubt notice the glass walls, but what you have not witnessed is that all of our meeting areas, every office, including mine, are also completely transparent. We want to encourage collaboration amongst the colleagues every day.' He gestured enthusiastically. 'It gives me great pleasure to say we have unified several sites, allowing scientists to talk face to face more regularly. Though knowing scientists, they might not enjoy this so much, no?'

There was a titter from the audience.

'You may have also noticed the curved walls, the lack of angles. This magnificent staircase linking each floor with the next.' He beamed, gesturing towards the elaborate spiral staircase in the centre. Rumours were the staircase had cost more than the entire building. It had been constructed entirely of pine, to reflect Mayer's Austrian heritage. 'Memory cannot be measured in straight lines; it is transient, ever changing. And science is the same, we recognise our research, constantly needs to evolve, no?'

Zach noticed several people nodding in agreement in the audience. He swallowed deeply from his glass, it was his third and he was feeling a pleasant warm numbness. He checked his pocket, felt the thick paper between his fingertips. His notes. Still there.

'Lastly,' Mayer continued, 'harmony. We are aware of the environmental challenges affecting our planet. When we built this new centre we ensured it is completely ecologically viable. Eco friendly, sustainable materials were used in its construction and our power is completely fuelled by recyclable waste.

This centre has created over one hundred new jobs. With this increase in employees, all working together in this one site, we hope that it will enable us to come closer to our overall goal. To find a cure for Tilder's Disorder.'

The Green Indian Problem

Synopsis

In a South Wales valley, in 1989, lives 7-year old JADE WATERS, known to his friends as 'GREEN'. Green just wants to play football and have a proper haircut, but he's an ordinary boy with an extraordinary problem, everyone thinks he's a girl. His parents think he will grow out of the tomboy behaviour, but he insists that there has been a big mistake, and he is a real boy.

When his classmates quiz him about his long hair and skirt, he comes up the 'the Indian lie' in an effort to explain his appearance. In trouble at school and at home, Green decides to do some detecting, like the men in the films he watches with his GRANDAD. Questioning his identity, he sets out on a mission to uncover the truth about who he is.

Meanwhile, Green has other problems. His mum LINDA has gone into zombie mode because she's sad. He's battling the evil DENNIS (his mum's abusive boyfriend), and his grandad has been diagnosed with terminal cancer. Life for Green gets darker still when his best friend MICHAEL goes missing. When Michael is found dead in the 'black bog', Green is heartbroken. His problem-solving skills are employed again, this time to find out what really happened to Michael. He puts his personal mystery on hold and decides to do some real detective work.

Green follows the police and attempts to find Michael's killer as he tries to make sense of the tragedy. He learns that everybody has their own mysteries and secrets, and he's not the only one with a problem. Green finds the evidence that will eventually frame the murderer, Michael's (Fake) UNCLE GARY. The mystery of Michael's death is uncovered, but Green's personal problem remains unsolved.

The Green Indian Problem
1989
Trees

Mrs R told us to make a family tree. She said a family tree is a type of drawing that is like a map of our families. She said we had to write names next to the people we drew. She also told us to write F or M next to the names. This means male or female.

My family tree is hard to do because some of my family are living with the wrong people. I drew a lot of trees. I put myself, my mum and my sister in the first tree. Then I put my dad, Tina, and my brothers in the second one. I put everybody else in the last trees.

Because I am in the top group and the teacher thinks I'm clever, she lets me write stories when I have finished my work. I don't think I'm that clever because I don't understand how spaceships work, and I am still trying to do my Rubik's cube. My dad can do it really quickly, but I can only get one side the same colour. Orange. If I am not working on a story, Mrs R sometimes tells me to go and sit with Michael and help him with his work. She says that Michael needs extra help. I know this is true because Michael does not understand that 2 x 2 is 4 or 3 + 4 is 7. Michael has also been writing his name wrong. He has been writing Micel. Then the other day I showed him how to write it. He copied his name out loads of times and now he can do it right.

Michael is my best friend. He lives in the next street to me, and he is allowed to stay out on his bike when I am in bed. He is also allowed to go outside without shoes. Michael lives with his mum and dad, his brother, his sister, and his dogs. He only drew one tree. There were too many people in it because he drew his whole family, even his aunties and uncles were dangling on the branches. He put the dogs at the bottom of it too. It looked like they had scared his family, so they climbed away. When I had finished my trees, I helped him to spell out the names in his family. I know how to spell all the names in mine.

I live with my mum, my little sister Verity and a horrible man called Den. Den is short for Dennis. I didn't put Den in our tree in the picture because he does not really belong there. He is so horrible he should have his own tree with no other people in it. I wish he was stuck in a tree and could never climb down. There should be special trees for people like Den.

My dad is called Graham, but everyone calls him Gray or Grayo. My mum is called Linda, and people just call her Linda. I wrote down all my dad's names on the branches of his tree. I put his new family in the tree with him too. My dad lives with a woman called Tina, and my two brothers, Aaron and Kai. When Mrs R was teaching us about families she said that some people can have half brothers and sisters. She said half brothers or sisters only share a mum or a dad, not both. She said it means only having one parent that is the same as each other. It was a bit confusing. Michael kept saying, 'I dunno what she's on about.' If Mrs R is right that would mean my brothers and sister are halves, but I think that is just stupid because you can't have half a sister. Sisters are not like fractions.

I wish my dad would live with us, but my mum said sometimes mums and dads can't stay with each other because they do not like to live together in the same house. I think they should check if they like to be around each other before they get married. I think that will save people from getting sad. I am sad because my dad does not live with us, but I am also sad because I am stuck.

Mrs R said if we get stuck we should try to work things out. She told us to do it on paper like we do in maths if we can't work out a sum. Then she gave us a spare workbook each, just for working things out. She said writing things down helps to work out problems. That is why I am writing this out. It's because I am stuck with things. When you are stuck, it is called a problem or a puzzle, and it can sometimes be called a mystery. My problem is a mystery because something has happened to me that I don't understand and I can't work out why it has happened. The teachers say if we try, but we still can't work out the answer to something we should ask somebody, but I don't know who will know the right answer. I want to work out the mystery by myself, but I think I will have to ask some questions to get some clues. That is what I am going to do. I am writing this down in the green workbook, so it is going to be my clue book as well as my working out book. I think it might take a long time to get the right answer because it is a very mysterious mystery.

Indians
When my dad asked me why I told the other kids in my class that I come from an Indian tribe, I didn't answer. I knew exactly why I said it, but I didn't tell him the truth because even though I am 7 and a half and he is 29, I know he doesn't understand because he keeps telling me a different thing is true. Instead of explaining, I decided to just be quiet. It was because I didn't know how to explain and also because I was afraid of crying in front of him.

'You're not a boy,' he said. 'You're not a bloody Indian either.'

His voice wasn't shouting, but his face was.

I didn't say anything.

'You're my little girl,' he said.

In my brain I could hear screaming. It was saying, 'NO I'M NOT! NO I'M NOT! NO I'M NOT!'

I ignored the inside shouting and I just let my dad say it. I didn't cry until he walked me home. I got sadder and sadder when I was watching him walk away down the street. Then he disappeared around the corner, and I cried because I knew he couldn't see me. I was sad that he was angry about the lie because I always want to please him because he's my dad. I cried because I know I am a disappointment. Disappointed is when you wish something was different or better. It is very hard to spell. I also cried because I want to be happy and I don't want to wear the skirt to school. The skirt is the reason I lied, and the skirt is my nemesis. We learned the word nemesis in class. It's easy to understand because all you have to do is think about superheroes. Lex Luthor is Superman's nemesis, and Darth Vader is Luke Skywalker's nemesis (even though really he's his dad).

The skirt is the thing I hate most in the whole world. I hate it more than Marmite and fish fingers. I even hate it more than Barbie dolls and *The Sound of Music*. *The Sound of Music* is a film, and it's the most boring one I have ever seen. I would rather not have a telly than watch it. I would rather look at the wall. The skirt means the other kids in my class think I'm a girl, I am not a girl though. I keep telling them that I'm not a girl, but I don't think they understand because they just look at me with goldfish style faces. The teachers don't understand either. They think I'm a girl too. This is because my mum and dad told them I am, and teachers never think that parents lie or get things wrong. When I tell the teachers I am a boy they give me a row and say, 'Don't be silly' and 'Behave' and 'Stop telling lies'. When I tell the other kids in my class, they just listen or stare. Sometimes they ask me lots of questions too.

'You can't be a boy because you've got long hair,' Gareth said.

I told him that lots of boys have long hair.

'Like who?' he said.

'Like pirates, wrestlers, Indians and Ozzy Osbourne,' I said.

'Who's Ozzy Osbourne?'

I told him that Ozzy Osbourne is a singer and he has got long hair, but he didn't know who I was talking about. I know Ozzy Osbourne because of my dad. I don't think Gareth's dad listens to Ozzy Osbourne, so I tried to think of someone he would know.

'Gazza used to have long hair,' I said.

Then Louise said, 'Well, why do you wear a skirt if you're a boy?'

That was when I made up the Indian lie. I told everyone I come from an Indian tribe. I am sticking to the Indian tribe story even though it is a risk, and my dad might find out again, and I might have another row. I have to stick to the Indian story because it explains why I have long hair and why I am not allowed to wear trousers, and I can't tell the truth because I am seven and a half and I don't even know what the truth is, that is why I am trying to work it out because it is a mystery. I don't even know why they make me do it. All I know is I am a boy, but everyone keeps telling me I'm not.

My mum does not stick to making me do girl things as much as everyone else. She does make me have some girl things, but she is the one who lets me have the most normal things and gives me a break from the skirt on the weekends. I love my mum and I want to please her but I do less to please her than the others. I think it is because I am with my mum most of the time and I find it hard to keep up pretending that everything is okay when I am at home.

My mum always looks sad, but not as sad as some other people, like Africans, on the telly. When she smiles she looks very nice. Sometimes I think my mum is sad because of me. I know that she was sad when Mrs R told her about the Indian lie, and I know she was sad when she realized I was sad about the skirt, but sometimes I have seen her get quite happy. One of the times she is happy is when her sister, my Auntie Carol, comes to visit from London. They go crazy when they see each other. They do the same laugh and anybody who is there can't help laughing because it is very funny to hear two women doing a crazy hyena laugh at the exact same time.

Green
Green is my favourite colour. When I had to choose a workbook, I chose green. There weren't many colours, so it was easy. You could pick either green or red. I like green because it is the colour of grass. There's lots of grass where I live because there are a lot of mountains. I also like green because I am Green. That is what I want my name to be, even though it is not really. I wish everybody would call me it, but they won't. My friends call me Green because that is what I like to be called. I like to be called Green for lots of reasons. It feels comfy when people say it, and it feels like it's the name I was supposed to have. It matches up with me. Green is what my real name means, but I don't like to be called my real name because it is a name for girls, and it makes me sad and embarrassed. Embarrassed is when you're sad and what to hide about something. Mrs R taught us that. I am embarrassed when people call me these words.
Her
She
Girl
My real name: JADE WATERS.

My friends didn't always call me Green. When I was even smaller, I had to be called my real name all the time. I started getting called Green when we played the game Boy, Girl, Fruit, Colour, in the yard at school. Louise put my real name in the girl list, and I crossed it out and changed it. I put it in the colour list instead. I did it because jade is a type of green, so it wasn't even a lie. My mum said different types of the same colour are called shades. I am a shade of green.

After the game, they called me Green, and it made me feel better, and now I am sticking to it, and when I grow up, I will change my name to Green forever. I'm going to keep my surname though. I'm going to be Green Waters because that is who I really am. I have written **Green** inside this workbook. I have written my address too, in case I lose it, then maybe someone will post it back to me. They might even read it and have ideas about my mystery. They might even work it out and tell me the answer.

Biographies

Judge's Biography

Emma Healey grew up in London where she studied for her first degree in bookbinding. She then worked for two libraries, two bookshops, two art galleries and two universities, before completing an MA in Creative Writing at the University of East Anglia. Her first novel, *Elizabeth is Missing*, was published to critical acclaim in 2014, became a *Sunday Times* bestseller, won the Costa First Novel Award and has recently been made into a BBC film. Her second novel, *Whistle in the Dark* was published in 2018. She lives in Norwich with her husband, daughter and cat.

Writers' Biographies

Jeff Adams was brought up in the mining village of Aberfan and his first job included a year underground at Deep Navigation colliery, mid Glamorgan. He joined the Royal Navy in 1965 and moved to Swindon after demobilisation. He has a keen interest in foreign and ancient languages and has held a variety of jobs including temporary crematorium assistant and warehouse worker for Books Club Associates. In 2010 he was the runner up for Ottakers (Cirencester) Poetry Competition. Whilst working on another novel, he became concerned no novel existed about the Aberfan Disaster, so decided to do something about it.

Tatum Anderson has worked as a journalist for over 20 years, with articles appearing in international science and medical publications. She wrote her first novel, *Bad Material*, while completing an MA in Creative Writing at Birkbeck, University of London. The manuscript has been shortlisted for the BPA First Novel Award 2020. Tatum's first published creative non-fiction piece, *The Invisibles*, appeared at the Waterloo Festival this year. *Mengo Baby* is Tatum's second novel. In the autumn, she will begin a PhD at Birkbeck on fiction in a post-truth era. She lives in South London with her family.

J M Briscoe is the pen name of stay-at-home-mum Jenny Wonnacott from Wokingham, Berkshire. Jenny is a trained journalist with experience in local newspaper and radio reporting, online and b2b trades magazines, however her true passion has always been writing fiction. In 2016 her unpublished Young Adult novel, *The Thing About Amelia,* was longlisted for the Mslexia Children's Novel Competition. Jenny wrote *The Girl with the Green Eyes* whilst pregnant with her third child in 2018/19 and edited it during the 2020 coronavirus lockdown whilst juggling childcare and home-schooling. She writes a light-hearted parenting blog called *Insert Future Here*. Website: http://jmbriscoe.com

Spencer Butler studied Architecture before joining BBC Television in London as a production designer. This led to directing in the theatre and, most recently, to a Creative Writing course with the Open University. Since then he has been writing full-time; completing two stage plays, two screenplays, the libretto for an oratorio, and a collection of short stories. Since completing his first novel, *Pegwell Bay*, he has written a second, *The Years*, and is currently in the process of researching a third, *Florence/Benin*. Spencer lives in West Dorset with his partner, the painter Paul Sinodhinos, and their gorgeous Norfolk terrier, Stella.

Mel Fraser is a freelance TV casting and drama producer with a diverse media portfolio, including primetime documentaries, music concerts and entertainment shows. She casts actors for TV roles in addition to short films and commercials. She's also scripted for presenters and worked as a writer/story editor for brand-sponsored series'. When she's not recon-structing the heinous crimes of notorious murderers or WW2 conflicts for TV, she writes poetry and scripts. Her first comedy script was selected for development and her next comedy script was longlisted by the BBC. *Gaslighters* is her first novel.

Michael Gallacher studied Literature and Philosophy in university and is currently a chef. He has also been telemarketer, tech support agent, market researcher, Greenpeace canvasser, thrift store manager and other less interesting characters like seller of cheap plastic toys on the street from a cardboard box. After spending most of his life in Canada, Michael moved back to the land of sires, and lives now in Glasgow, Scotland where he loves the weather.

Carole Hailey abandoned a lucrative career as a lawyer to become an impoverished novelist after years of failing to write in the middle of the night. She subsequently accumulated an MA in Creative Writing from Goldsmiths, University of London and a PhD from Swansea University. Drawing comfort from all the writers who have at least two unpublished novels languishing in a drawer, *The Silence Project* is Carole's third novel, but the first to be longlisted for a prize. Carole is a 2020/21 London Library Emerging Writer. You can find her on Twitter: @CaroleAHailey

Jessica Harneyford turned to writing after working as an advisor to technology companies. *The Improbable Case of the Being in the Robot* is influenced by this experience, and by her studies in psychology and linguistics. She developed the concept for the novel during a residency with interactive media artists *Blast Theory*. An earlier version, *My Artificial Rose*, was shortlisted in the MsLexia 2018 Novella competition. Jessica also writes non-fiction and poetry. Her articles have been published in *How We Get to Next* and she was a prize-winner in the Apples & Snakes / Nuffield Council on Bioethics (un)natural competition. Twitter: @jharneyford

Carla Jenkins was born in Essex, went to school in Norfolk, and taught English as a foreign language in London and Madrid before settling in Devon. She worked as a secondary school English teacher before deciding to follow a long-held dream of completing an MA in Creative Writing which she is currently studying for at Exeter University. She runs courses and workshops focusing on creative writing for wellbeing. During Lockdown, Carla signed up for a writing course at The Novelry and wrote *Fifty Minutes*, her first novel.

Margaret Jennings has been writing for many years and has an MA in Creative Writing. Her poetry anthology, *We Are the Lizards*, was recently published by Dempsey and Windle. It's available at dempseyand-windle.com/margaret-jennings.html. A published short story writer, Margaret is working on her second novel, *Ten Tricks*. She was longlisted for the Bare Fiction Literary short story prize 2014 and has been shortlisted in The Bridport Prize for flash fiction. Her work has featured in numerous anthologies and been performed by theatre companies. Margaret enjoys spoken word events and is an active member of the Portsmouth writing community.

Peter Lewenstein was a journalist specialising in African affairs before he switched to fiction, since when he's written three novels about the exploits of human rights investigator Patrice Le Congo – of which *Burned* is the latest. The first, *Skinned*, was longlisted for the Bridport Prize for a First Novel in 2017. The second, *Grabbed*, was longlisted for the Crime Writers' Association's Debut Dagger award in 2018. Peter also writes short stories and attends Creative Writing courses at Morley College in London. He lives in London. When not writing, he does normal things like walking the dog and watching football.

Alan MacGlas is a former government servant and current professional editor of poetry and stories. Having gained the necessary skills for writing fiction in the preparation of briefs and correspondence for ministers and senior colleagues, he has published one book of miscellaneous articles, stories, poems and bagatelles (*The Collected Homework of Albert Gulliver Trumpshaw*) and one pamphlet of serious poetry (*Mortal Clay*). He was winner of the 2019 *'To Hull and Back'* humorous short story competition. www.christopherfielden.com

Tracy Maylath came of age in Littleton, Colorado before her high school, Columbine, tragically made a name of the innocuous suburb. Adopting London as her home, she then achieved two MAs in Creative Writing; from Goldsmiths and from the University of East Anglia. Her story *The Laughter of Jackhammers* came runner-up in The Guardian Summer Short Story Award in 2010, *Troll* was shortlisted for the Bridport Flash Fiction Award and she's had two short stories longlisted for the Fish Publishing Prize. She is now channelling her love of drag queens into her novel set in a seemingly innocuous American suburb.

Maurice McBride was born and raised in northern England and read Engineering at King's in London. Throughout his career in the construction industry (rising to Board Director) he also indulged his passions for writing and travelling. Having seen much of the West, his fascination with the East took him to China (including Kashgar), India, Vietnam, Cambodia, Syria, Iran, and Uzbekistan. In his writing, he believes in providing the reader with memorable characters, an original and occasionally humorous narrative voice, vivid settings and – above all else – *story*. He lives on the Hampshire-Berkshire border with his family and a mongrel dog with too much personality.

Rob Perry grew up in Norfolk but currently lives in the Peak District where he works as a weightlifting coach. He is a graduate of the UEA creative writing BA. In 2019 he was selected for the National Centre for Writing's Escalator programme. He's been shortlisted for the Bridport Short Story Prize, the Bristol Short Story Prize and the Fish Short Story Prize. He won the Nottingham Short Story Prize and was first runner-up in the Moth International Short Story Prize and The Winston Fletcher

Memorial Prize. George Saunders is his absolute hero. *Dog* is his first novel.

Joseph Pierson has a PhD in Creative Writing from Kingston University. His stories have been published in *Ambit, Litro, Minor Literature[s]* and *Shooter Magazine*.

Julia Rampen, born in Edinburgh, used to think Cumbria was the south of England until she moved to London in her twenties, where she became a journalist and editor, with stints at *The Mirror* and *New Statesman*. Now based at the *Liverpool Echo*, she regularly writes on social affairs and politics. She was a Foyle Young Poet of the year in 2005 and 2006 and the co-founder of the Syrian storytelling blog, Qisetna: Talking Syria. In addition to the Bridport longlist, her draft novel has been shortlisted for the First Pages and Bath Novel awards.

Gordon Scott is married, has two daughters, and lives partly in Belfast, partly in Spain. He is an early-retired finance director, has attended creative writing courses and is now writing full-time. In 2018, he achieved the longlist, shortlist, and was awarded second place in the final judging of Hastings Litfest. (A submission extract from previous work.) *Sins of the Fathers* is the second novel in an unpublished series featuring private detective, Mike Madagan. Outside of writing, Gordon enjoys reading, walking, travelling, and is a keen rock guitarist.

Michelle Shinn grew up in Essex, before heading North to complete a degree in English. After being diagnosed with breast cancer in 2016, Michelle rekindled her love for writing with a personal blog charting the highs and lows of this life changing experience. Currently studying an MA in Creative Writing at Manchester Metropolitan University, her short story, *Finding Treasure*, was highly commended in the Manchester Fiction Prize. Now immersed in the Manchester creative writing community, Michelle is a regular attendee at the South Manchester Writer's Workshop. She works in marketing to fund her passion for travelling to escape the rain! Twitter: @michelleshinn_

Jack Leaf Willetts is a writer from Llanbradach, a strange, beautiful village in South Wales. At university, he studied English Literature and graduated with dreams of being a writer. He has had poetry published by *Empty Mirror*, *PoV* magazine, and Unknown Press. His writing focuses on the beauty and heartbreak of everyday life and extraordinary characters in ordinary worlds. All his stories are available for adaptation, should Wes Anderson be interested. Jack is currently working on a coming of age follow up to *The Green Indian Problem*. You can find him on Twitter @JackLeafWrites